Refugee - Text copyright © Emmy Ellis 2023
Cover Art by Emmy Ellis @ studioenp.com © 2022

All Rights Reserved

REFUGEE

Emmy Ellis

Chapter One

Zoe Callaghan, an ex-worker on Debbie's corner, now a spy for George and Greg Wilkes, walked into their recent acquisition, Vintage Finds, via the back. The emporium was where she gave the meat and bones of information when messages either weren't enough or what she had to say was best kept off phones. Her current target, Macey Moorhouse, was a light-fingered bitch who'd stolen a necklace worth two grand from Vintage Finds last week. Karma, fate, or whatever you wanted to call it, someone had nicked the necklace off her, in the street of all places, and now Macey was down a grand, the price she'd been asking for it. The twins were after her—and the fella who'd done the nicking. He'd raced off in his poncy blue sports car, one George knew. Sadly, they hadn't found them yet, despite having people out searching.

"Only me," she called through the ajar internal door to the manager, Angie, slipping the keys in her handbag. She went over to the kettle in the staff-cum-storage room, lifting it to peer at the gauge on the side. "Bloody hell, it's empty." She filled it at the sink. Flicked it on. Slumped down on one of the comfy chairs to read Angie's latest magazine full of celebrity gossip.

According to the front page, a famous actor was having it away with a pretty little thing behind his wife's back. In a way, Zoe felt better that even the rich and famous did bad shit, that they were the same as everyone else, not these on-a-pedestal people who could do no wrong. Her boys' father, Pete, had cheated on her a long while ago, and it had taken months for her to get over it, but she was fine now, couldn't care less who he dipped his wick in so long as it wasn't her.

The kettle clicked off, and she got up. "Do you want tea, Angie?"

Zoe dumped leaves in the pot then poured on water. She popped the cosy on the top and, thinking Angie must be busy with customers, went out into the yard for a ciggie while the tea brewed. This was the life, working as her version of Miss Marple, following suspects, listening out for new ones. She got paid well, and the only blot on her landscape was ferrying her two teens to and from school, although to be fair, she could ditch doing that as they'd asked her yesterday if they could take the bus. She supposed they could, they didn't need mollycoddling anymore, and so long as they came straight home, texting her they'd arrived safely, she reckoned she could cope with that.

The problem was, she'd been frightened in the past, so she was a bit protective when it came to her lads. Pete had turned up at the school when they'd been nine and ten. He'd taken them, not checking with her first, and off they'd gone to McDonald's, while she'd stood outside their classroom, thinking they'd been kidnapped by 'a man in a black beanie hat', as he'd been described by another mother. As the school usually didn't let children go with anyone who wasn't on 'the list', Zoe had crapped herself that some random paedo had whisked them away, pretending to be Pete. She'd phoned to tell him they had an abduction on their hands; never in her life had she imagined she'd say those words.

He'd laughed and said, "They're with me, you silly cow."

"How was *I* supposed to fucking know that?" she'd screeched, getting a funny look off someone for swearing in front of the nearby kids. She'd lowered her voice. "Don't you ever, *ever* take them without telling me first. I thought they'd been nabbed!"

She'd cried with relief then, big racking sobs that had garnered even more attention, pitying stares, either because she'd lost her cool in public or the mothers had empathy for what she'd just been through.

She blinked back the tears; they always sprouted with that memory. God, Pete was such a dickhead when it came to their sons. Well, if she was being *really* honest, when it came to her. She was sure he did this sort of thing on purpose to hurt her. Weird, that, because *she* was the wronged party, it had been *him* who'd broken their wedding vows, not to mention all that secret gambling and generally talking to and treating her like shit. She supposed it had got worse because she'd had the cheek (his words) to kick him out once she'd discovered what he'd been up to. Pete wouldn't have expected her to love herself enough to do that. Well, she deserved more than him, and she'd acted accordingly to safeguard her future emotional state. Better to cut him off at the knees than give him carte blanche to do it again later down the line, his 'sorry' meaning nothing. She'd have been even more hurt then.

"Not on your nelly," she mumbled, smoke chuntering out around the words. "Fucking moron."

With her, it was one strike and you're out these days, although she was lenient with the kids. They were entitled to make mistakes and be forgiven, that was all part of growing up. Pete, though, no. Since that day, she'd had his name

5

taken off the school's general pickup list, and he was only allowed to collect them if she told the teachers it had been arranged and she was fine with it. He hadn't liked that, and you'd think he'd learn, wouldn't you, that she wasn't brooking any argument, but time and again he did stuff to naff her off, and time and again she blocked it so whatever trick he'd played couldn't be repeated.

Twat. She reckoned he had a few brain cells missing if he hadn't spotted the pattern yet. Still, he was the least of her worries, a minor irritation, no one worth getting narked about, and he'd been behaving better lately as he had a new missus, Genevieve, although he'd seemed to think, when he'd told Zoe about her, that she was meant to be upset. Jealous. Err, no.

She finished her fag and returned indoors to poke her head around the door into the shop. Angie wasn't behind the counter, nor was she stocking up the shelves that held all manner of vintage items. Had she nipped out into the high street? Zoe glanced at the front door. The sign pointing towards her said OPEN, so CLOSED faced the other way for the customers. Hmm, it *was* lunchtime, and Angie was entitled to take her break elsewhere.

Zoe stepped into the three-aisle emporium, conscious of the cameras that would track her every move. Since Macey had stolen the necklace, the twins had upped security. You couldn't breathe in here without CCTV picking it up. She walked down the first aisle that led to the front door, peering into the street at the shoppers. Ants, they were, scurrying about, on a mission, bags hanging at the crooks of arms, one bloke hefting along a big box containing a seventy-inch flatscreen, his eyes peering over the top. She shook her head. That was something Pete would do, carrying it instead of parking up round the back of Argos and putting it straight in the motor.

She turned and walked up the middle aisle, staring ahead at the glass counter, and her heart stuttered, her skin going cold. Oh God, it had been smashed, all of the jewellery missing. She rushed forward over the chunks of broken glass, taking in the spiderweb cracks surrounding the jagged hole. Every single item was gone bar a set of earrings that must have been ignored in the thief's rush to get out.

Where the hell was Angie? Had the robber only just done this before Zoe had arrived? Or, Jesus Christ, had it happened when she'd been smoking? She spun round and went back to the front door, peering at the gap to see the Yale keeper firmly in place, plus the one for the mortice lock lower down. So Angie must have gone out, secured the place, *after* the robbery? Or had it already been locked and the thief had entered through the back, like Zoe had?

Christ, that door had been open, so…

Something at the end of aisle three, the last in the line, caught her attention. She turned slowly, dreading seeing a rat—there had been a few living here before the twins had renovated it. It wasn't a rat but hands on the floor. Nausea paid Zoe a visit, and she swallowed, fear creeping up inside her.

"Angie?" That had come out broken, as if Zoe had a sore throat. "Is that you?"

What if it wasn't? What if it was a customer, or even worse, the robber who just waited for her to round the corner, then she'd get shot? Stabbed?

"Fucking hell," she whispered and took her phone out of her pocket. She flicked her attention from her screen and back to the hands several times while she accessed the twins' number. She listened to it ring, inching closer to whoever it was. At aisle three, at the end rack filled with strange and wonderful paraphernalia, she poked her head round.

Oh fuck. Oh my bloody fuck…

"All right, Zoe?" George asked.

She jumped at hearing his voice in her ear. "Angie…it's Angie."

"Don't piss about. I recognise your voice. It's Zoe."

"No, yes, I mean… It's me, but Angie… Someone's robbed Vintage, and she's…she's on the floor, covered in blood. She…she looks dead… They must have done it while I was out the back having a fag. Help me. Please, for fuck's sake, come and help me…"

She sank to the floor, her back against the wall below the display window, staring at Angie's chest. It didn't rise and fall. No breath ghosted between her parted lips. Her eyes didn't crinkle at the sides like they usually did whenever she saw Zoe and smiled. Instead, they stared at her.

Angie lay on her side, her knees bent, the soles of her shoes butted against the bottom of the aisle shelving. Her arms, cable tied at the wrists, stuck straight out in front of her, fingers relaxed. Blood spattered the body of her white T-shirt, but a bib of it ruined the chest area. Zoe, her breathing erratic, gawped at Angie's throat. A dark line ran across it, and blood oozed from it onto the floor, a slow seep, a puddle of red. Angie's blonde hair soaked it up, a few tendrils that had come loose from her skewwhiff topknot, the usually neat bun ruined, perhaps by someone grabbing it and dragging Angie from behind the counter. The fear she must have gone through…

The twins would know exactly what had happened once they viewed the footage, unless Angie had been forced to switch it off. Zoe tore her gaze away from Angie and peered at the camera pointing her way. It looked all right, didn't seem to have been tampered with, the lens still intact. She prayed whoever had done this had been caught on film, then The Brothers could go after them, sort them, get justice for poor Angie who wouldn't have hurt a fly. She was fifty-something, no harm to anyone, and had always banged on about her grandkids, two girls who loved their nanny to distraction. God, fancy them finding out she'd been murdered at work. They were only five and seven. It was bound to scar them for life.

The key going in the lock had Zoe screaming. She was that wound up, her reaction had come from being scared out of her mind. She scrabbled to get up, her brain catching on—*a key, so it has to be the twins*. She glanced that way. George and Greg stood side by side at the end of aisle one, grey suits, white shirts, red ties, no beards or fake glasses today.

"She's…" Zoe swallowed. "She's had her throat slit, and her wrists are tied."

Greg shut the door using his elbow. He sighed and looked at George. "We can't hide this."

"No." George shook his head. "But we can get Janine to come out rather than phone nine-nine-nine."

"I'll do it." Greg walked into the back room.

George came over and held a hand out. "Up you get. You're contaminating a crime scene."

She took his hand and stood. Glanced at Angie. "Fuck, oh fuck…"

"Don't look at her. You'll give yourself nightmare fodder. Come out the back while we wait for the police. They'll want to speak to you, obviously."

"Do I tell them about Macey and the necklace, the bloke in the sports car?"

"No, you just say what went on today."

He led the way out the back, still holding her hand. The door was open, Greg outside on the phone. George pushed her onto the chair she'd so recently sat on, when life had been a case of annoying herself with thoughts of Pete and diving into the sordid world of the celebrities between the pages of a magazine she never wanted to read again.

"Why am I here, though?" she asked George. "I mean, what do I tell the police? I walked straight in. They'll see that from the outside footage."

"You were coming for an interview, hence why we were already on our way here when you rang. I don't want the plods knowing you already work for us. I want you kept out of this as much as possible."

"But I made a pot of tea."

"So? I'll say we told you to make yourself at home. Stop fretting. It's Janine and her DS who'll arrive first. She's on our books, but the DS fella hasn't got a clue, understand?"

Zoe nodded. Jesus, working for The Brothers was a risk she'd been prepared to take, she'd needed the money and a way out of opening her legs for a living, but now? With Angie dead?

What if whoever had killed her knew Zoe came to Vintage every day? What if they'd been watching the shop, staking it out to know when to strike? What if they'd seen her going to the front door and looking out just now? They might come after her, want to shut her up.

She blurted all that to George, needing to get her fears off her chest. "I've got my kids to think of. What if the robber's clocked me and followed me home before now? They could be waiting at mine."

George took a deep breath. "We'll check the CCTV now, see if you recognise them as someone you've seen around at any point. Whether you've clocked them before or not, we'll keep you and your children safe until we find them."

Feeling marginally better about that, Zoe relaxed a tad. There was no way she'd let her boys get the bus until this was all over. She'd never put them in the firing line. They were her life, and without them, she'd be nothing.

She thought about the murder happening while she'd been chugging on her ciggie. And shuddered.

Chapter Two

George stared, mouth hanging, at the CCTV screen. Was he seeing straight? There was the hairstyle to consider, which wasn't right and probably a wig, but the face, despite the person having a Zorro mask on, was familiar. "That fucking bitch…"

He couldn't get over the balls of her. Macey fucking Moorhouse with some bloke in a balaclava, standing in Vintage at the counter around the time Zoe had entered via the back, Angie behind it, her hands raised. The fella held a shotgun, pointing it at Angie. They must have told her to keep quiet until Zoe had gone outside. Macey stared at the glass counter, a ruddy great smile on her chops as if what was happening was *normal*.

"Slag," Greg said beside him.

"Who is it?" Zoe asked from her chair.

"Macey," George said. "She's got a wig and mask on but failed to hide that beauty spot of hers, or her teeth, which are distinctive because of her overbite. What a div."

"Bloody hell," Zoe said. "I know she's the sort who doesn't give a shit, but this kind of robbery, and *murder*?"

"Hmm, just goes to show appearances can be deceptive." George continued to watch the robbery take place, the fella smashing the counter glass and Macey stuffing her gloved hand inside the hole, grabbing the jewellery and dropping it into her oversized handbag. "There was us lot, thinking she was a common or garden shoplifter, when she's clearly got her sights set higher."

On the screen, Angie reached towards the underside of the counter, likely to press the red button that sent an alert directly to the police. The man wafted the gun at her, leaning forward to say something, and Angie made her way round the side of the counter. She held her hands out, wrists pressed together, and Macey used a cable tie to secure them.

Angie ran down aisle three in an attempt to escape.

George switched to another camera.

Balaclava went after Angie. He struck the back of her head with the butt of the shotgun, and she went sprawling, her face smacking onto the floor. He propped the gun against the shelving then fished in his pocket. Brought something out and flicked his wrist. A knife.

"Bastard," George muttered.

"What's happening now?" Zoe asked.

"You don't want to know, love." Greg sighed. "Whoever he is, we're going to end him. Prison's too good for him."

George changed the view to a camera above the window at the end of aisle three. Balaclava wrenched Angie's head back and sliced her throat. George stared, fascinated, as the skin

17

parted and blood gushed. Then, for reasons only known to himself, Balaclava arranged her body in the position Zoe had found her in. He slipped the knife away, picked up the gun, then returned to the counter, going behind it.

George switched cameras again.

Balaclava opened a drawer, held up a set of keys, and made for the front door. George toggled between views. Macey ran down aisle two and turned to stand at the end of three. She stared at Angie, hands going to her wig, and she clutched it, her mouth opening in what George imagined was either a scream or silent, gawping shock.

Balaclava left the shop, and Macey followed. The man locked the door, and they got into what appeared to be the sports car George and Greg had been trying to find since Macey had stolen the necklace. The vehicle sped off. George checked the outside camera to see what shoppers had done at this point. No one appeared alarmed at two masked people, one with a bloody shotgun, for fuck's sake, leaving Vintage. They were in a world of their own, intent on getting their shopping done. London was an eclectic place full of some whacky people, but surely their masks were an obvious pointer that screamed: *Robbery!*

"Look at them," he said. "Toddling along as if nothing's happened."

Greg tutted. "You can't blame people for having tunnel vision, being lost in their heads. Half of them can't pay their electric and gas bills—they've got more on their minds than what other people are up to, like how to eat tonight, next week, next month."

"True."

George got on with copying the footage onto a USB stick he found in the desk drawer, ready to give to Janine. Greg had told her to come round the back, and she was taking her sweet time, considering this was murder they were dealing with.

"Is it bad to drink that tea Zoe made while we wait?" George asked.

Greg tsked. "It'll be well stewed by now, and it's best we don't touch anything."

George didn't like not being allowed to do something in his own property, but he conceded the point. This side of things was Janine's domain now, but the other part, where Macey and Balaclava got hunted down, was theirs.

A knock at the back door, and Janine opened it and stuck her head in. "Do your cameras have audio?"

"No."

"Good, then we can talk freely. I managed to come without the DS. Told him to meet me here in half an hour, so be quick and tell me the real deal before he gets here." She pushed the door wide, booties over her feet, gloves on, and a forensic suit covering her slim body.

"Good." George gestured for her to come in. "You've said he's a nosy twat. We could do without having to watch what we say. Could do without having to give a statement to be honest, but the cameras have caught us turning up, so…" He took the USB out of the laptop. "It's all on tape. No idea who did it, though. They had masks on." He glanced at Zoe to shut her up before she even thought of opening her mouth.

"Right." Janine puffed air out, her cheeks ballooning. "Tell me what happened. Who found the body?"

"Aren't you going in there to check she's really dead?" Zoe asked.

"Is she likely to be with a cut throat?" Janine said to her. "Did you see any signs of life?"

"No." Zoe hugged herself.

Janine said, "A cut like that, she's not alive, but I'd best go and look if you've got cameras. Don't want to have the DCI up my arse, asking why I didn't do it."

She disappeared into the shop.

Zoe sniffed. "She looks a right hard cow."

"She can be," George said. "Mardy an' all, but she's good at what she does. She'll know we're gunning for Macey and that bloke, and she'll cover up whatever she needs to."

Janine came back to the door, remaining in the shop since she had blood on her booties. "Dead. So, out with it. What's your version of events?"

George held a hand out to Zoe. "You go first, love."

Zoe took a deep breath then recounted everything she'd done since entering the shop via the back.

"Do you work here, then?" Janine asked.

George filled her in on the unofficial story.

"Right." Janine rubbed her forehead with the back of her gloved hand. "We'll go with that. Saves muddying the waters."

They chatted for a while longer, until the DS turned up. He entered in forensic gear, got the gist from Janine, then walked into the shop to let SOCO in at the front, using George's keys.

George passed the USB stick to Janine. "That's for you. We'll nip to the station now to give our official statements. I can't be doing with a copper coming to our place. You know I like my privacy."

Janine nodded and smiled, a wicked gleam in her eyes. "You'll need to surrender your clothes and shoes."

George glared at her. "Are you taking the piss?"

"Nope. You were all at the crime scene. I'll get you some forensic gear to wear to the station." She winked. "You ought to be well used to those outfits, so stop staring at me like you want to cut my tongue out."

"I can't drive in bare feet," George said.

Janine held her middle finger up. "Then you'll have to learn, won't you."

The statements took three hours, and George was well and truly naffed off by the time they got home. Zoe was in a safe house with her sons, so she was well out of the way.

In the kitchen, George made Pot Noodles, taking out a mini packet of Tangtastics for pudding. He sliced some tiger bread, cutting enough for Greg, and buttered it, needing the comfort food, because being involved with the police in that way had him uneasy. They'd flown under the radar the whole time since they'd started running The Cardigan Estate, so to sit in a soft interview room and give an account of what had happened, having to provide an alibi, for fuck's sake… Thank God they'd come here in the BMW and not the fake work van or taxi. Did the copper suspect it was an insurance scam? Thankfully, they hadn't been up to anything dodgy that morning, and saying they'd been in The Angel having breakfast, then sat there for a while until they'd been due to meet Zoe at Vintage, had been taken as gospel. Or so George assumed.

They'd collected Zoe's boys from school, checked her house for anyone lurking inside, and allowed them to pack a bag each. Her lads thought it was because of the robbery, not because their mother had been following Macey around lately and could have been spotted. Then they'd sent the trio off with Will, one of their best men, in their taxi, and he'd stay with them so Zoe didn't feel afraid and abandoned.

Greg came in after having a shower, another grey suit on, another red tie. "I don't like the idea of pigs touching my clothes. I'll burn the bastards when we get them back." He sat at the island.

George took their food over and perched beside him on a stool. "Eat this, then we'll go scouting, get tougher when asking questions about where Macey is. She hasn't been at her flat for days."

"She's obviously staying somewhere else." Greg dipped folded bread into his noodles.

George did the same. "How the fuck's she got involved with Denny Rawlings?" He thought about the blue sports car owner. "Why did he snatch that necklace off her then take her to Vintage to steal our shit?" He bit off the sauce-soaked bread.

"Might not have been Denny. He could have let someone borrow his car."

"True, but they still have a connection to him. He was still stupid enough to allow his *distinctive* car to be used. D'you think he was sending us a message, that he *wants* us to know he's involved?"

Greg ate and chewed. Swallowed. "Maybe he's who Macey was on the phone to last week in Bumble's Café, when Zoe overhead her trying to flog the necklace. If you remember, Macey was a bit abrasive to whoever she spoke to, cocky, rude, and Denny wouldn't have liked that. He probably took the necklace to teach her a lesson. She might have got hold of him later to discuss what the fuck was going on, and they met up. Ever since, she hasn't been at home. Martin and Will haven't clocked her or the sports car while they've been outside her gaff, keeping watch, and no one seems to want to tell us where Denny lives. The electoral roll hasn't helped us either. He's got to pay council tax, yet his name's not down."

"Probably scamming the system."

"Do you think, when we went round to where his parents used to live, that the neighbour lied to us? He might well live there with someone, and it's their name that's down as the bill payer. Who was it again? Some woman…"

"Can't remember, but she checked out, so unless we've been duped…" George thought about Martin, sitting in a nondescript car, keeping an eye on Macey's place during the daytime shift. "We'll use the fake work van, drop some food to Martin. Also, we need to get someone to take over Will's night shift now he's at the safe house."

"I suppose that means me sorting it," Greg grumbled.

"Hmm."

They got on with the business of eating, then Greg sent a message to arrange for someone to relieve Martin later.

The trip to get food and go to Macey's street didn't take long, and George drew alongside Martin's car. Greg opened the passenger window, passed over a Burger King bag, then George drove away. Speaking would mean they were more likely to be spotted, so any talking would be done over the phone whenever Martin checked in.

"Where to now?" Greg asked.

"We'll go back to her local. We were in disguise last time, but *this* time I want the landlord to know who he's dealing with. No fucking about. I want Angie's killer caught. Strung up."

"You and me both."

George drove on and soon came to the Bassett Hound, a big pub that did food and had discos at the weekends until three a.m., a lively place by all accounts. They strode inside, pausing on the bristly mat in front of the door, eyeing up the customers. A few recognised them and made a show of looking innocent, while others acted as if having The Brothers in their vicinity was normal. George spotted Sonny Bates, who they'd instructed to sit here all day and listen out for gossip about Macey and to let them know if she came in. Jimmy Riddle, their other fella, propped the bar up at night.

George plonked his beady gaze bang on the landlord who widened his eyes then smiled, like they were old mates.

Creep.

George and Greg strutted up to the bar.

"Macey Moorhouse," George said quietly. "Been in lately, has she?"

The sign above the door had a typo stating the establishment sold 'bears' instead of 'beers' and that the landlord was Patrick Hart.

"A couple of fellas came in last week asking about her," Patrick said.

"Did they now." George wasn't about to say it had been them in disguise and Patrick was a dickhead for not recognising his voice. "Seems she's in demand. So, has she been in?"

"Not seen her in here for a good few days. Must be about eight or nine."

A nearby barmaid came over. Her name tag said NANCE beneath the word MANAGER. "She was in the weekend before last for the sixties disco. If you remember, Pat, she slapped a customer and had to be turfed out."

"Oh yeah," Patrick said, his head bobbing. "I told her if she didn't stop being lairy, she was barred. When she didn't come back in, I took it that she thought I'd *actually* barred her. She was so pissed up, she probably didn't hear me right."

"Can we have a word in private?" Greg asked.

George glanced at him. Greg spoke without words, as they sometimes had to, his eyes shifting left to right. Ah, he didn't think it was a good idea to let earwiggers know what was going on.

Patrick blinked. "Um, on my own?"

Greg smiled. "What d'you think we're going to do, duff you up? Give you a Cheshire? Why would we do that if you haven't done anything wrong?"

Patrick shrugged. "Well, you know, people talk about you two, and I don't want any trouble."

"You'll get it if you don't take us to an office or whatever," Greg said. "My patience is wearing thin, so get a move on."

George raised his eyebrows at his twin. What had crawled up *his* arse? Was he still hacked off about the police touching his precious clothes?

Patrick moved along the bar to raise the hatch, and George walked through, Greg following. Patrick led them to an office down a corridor, a nice and tidy one, the walls showcasing Patrick's certificates and accomplishments in black frames. Apparently, he sold his own brew here called Fairy's Arse.

Won't be drinking that, then…

The landlord sat behind the desk, probably to put something between them should Greg get narked again. Not that it would stop him from reaching over and gripping Patrick's collar.

George shut the door and stood beside his brother. "You pay us protection money."

"Yeah…"

"But that protection will be null and void if you don't tell us something that could help us track Macey down." George glared at him. "You'd know soon enough anyway, but I don't want you gossiping about this until it hits the news, got it?"

Patrick nodded. "Whatever you want." He gave Greg a nervous glance.

"Macey's in a spot of trouble." An understatement. George shoved a hand in his pocket. He needed Patrick to wonder if he was feeling for a gun. "She was involved in a robbery at our shop, and whoever she was with slit our manager's throat."

"Vintage Finds? Angie?" Patrick swallowed hard. "*What*? Oh shit. Oh fuck…"

George sensed there was more to this reaction. "What's the matter?"

"Angie's my sister-in-law."

Oh fuck, indeed. "Ah. Sorry you had to hear the news so bluntly." George may as well continue in that vein. "She's dead, by the way."

"Fuck. Oh, shitting hell." Patrick propped his elbows on the desk and put his face in his hands. "Liv's going to need me…"

"Your wife?"

"Yes…"

30

"I'd say sorry for pushing on with this little chat, but I'm not sorry, not when one of our employees has been killed. Anything you can tell me about Macey and Denny Rawlings—"

"Denny?" Patrick dropped his hands and stood, gripping his hair. "Was it *him*?"

"They left in his sports car, so we assume so."

"That fucking little cunt…" Patrick went to the frosted window and opened the top part, probably needing air as he'd broken out in a sweat. "He's… I've got something to tell you about him. I thought it was a rumour, bullshit, but…" He turned and faced them. "Even if it's bollocks, it's best you know now."

"Know what?" Greg asked, clenching his fists.

"He's apparently been taking in refugees."

George didn't see a problem with that. Denny had always given to charity, bigging up his persona, making out he was a good bloke when really he was an insufferable pain the backside who didn't seem to care whether the twins had told him to stop his dodgy dealings since they'd taken over. They'd never been able to prove he was still doing shit behind their backs, selling stuff from the boot of his car, but they suspected he did.

31

"So?" George said. "What's he doing, renting houses to them or something?"

"No. It's not his usual 'helping those in need' crap. Yes, he helps the homeless and whatever else he claims he does, but the refugees are different. Someone said he's buying them from whoever brings them over and they're trapped in the sex trade. Like I said, I thought it was rubbish, that he wouldn't stoop that low, but now he's killed Angie, who knows what he's capable of."

"Supposedly killed. All I said was they left in Denny's car. The fella had a balaclava on." Still, that was by the by, wasn't it? Especially in light of what Patrick had said. Buying refugees? Who the fuck did Denny think he was? "Who do we talk to about this? Point us in the right direction — and no, we won't say you sent us their way."

"Beaker."

"Pardon me?"

"Beaker, that's the fella's name." Patrick returned to his seat, leant back, and closed his eyes. "He's the one who told me about the refugees. He lives above the chippy round the corner." He opened his eyes again and rubbed them.

"What does he look like?"

"That *Muppet* character. Ginger hair, long face, big eyes."

"And his real name?"

"I don't know. Everyone calls him Beaker."

"Right." George glanced at Greg who nodded. "Remember, not a word to anyone about what we've discussed. You wait to hear about Angie from your wife, understand? You feign shock, whatever you need to do to disguise the fact you already knew." George took some cash from his inside suit pocket. He slapped it on the desk, the notes fanning out. "You're now our informant. Act accordingly."

George left the office, storming down the corridor and through the bar hatch. Outside, he thumbed a message to Sonny.

GG: Watch the landlord. See if he acts shifty.

Sonny: Will do.

Greg joined George, and they got in the van.

It was time to visit a scrote who could well give them all the answers they needed.

Chapter Three

Patrick went into the staff loo and stared at himself in the speckled mirror above the sink, some of the reflective stuff peeling off the corner. He made a mental note to replace it but had bigger issues to contend with at the minute. Jesus Christ, what was he going to do? He needed to get his ducks in a row, sharpish, think about what he'd just said and how he could extricate himself from anything sticky that might come his way. He was in deep enough as it was, and because of his big mouth, he'd gone even deeper. Soon, he'd be buried beneath rubble he could have prevented from toppling onto him. He was usually so calm, kept the two sides of his life in compartments, well away from each other, but they'd merged now, what with Angie's death, and he didn't like it. Oil and water mixing, that's what had happened, and his dealings with Denny were the oil and could be visible soon if he didn't take measures to sort it.

Bollocks. I don't need this.

He'd shit himself when the twins had come into the pub. The sight of them…well, he'd known it could only mean trouble. He'd had a feeling they'd sent two massive blokes to question him last week about Macey, but that time, Nance hadn't come over and dropped Macey's name into the equation. He could have killed her for doing it today. Then they'd gone into his office with him, and he'd been convinced they hadn't really been there regarding Macey but instead The Network, which was why, when Denny's name had been mentioned, he'd blamed knowing about it on Beaker and put Denny bang in the middle of the frame.

When they'd said about Denny, Patrick had panicked and reckoned it was better to send them in his direction than have the spotlight on himself, plus a rush of anger had surged through him at the possibility that Denny had gone on the robbery and killed Angie. That twat, Honda, was supposed to have been Macey's accomplice. Denny knew Angie was Patrick's sister-in-law, knew she wasn't supposed to be harmed when the gear was being nicked, yet she was *dead*! Plans must have been changed while Patrick wasn't there.

He'd visited the shop when Angie had first started running it for the twins so knew the layout. He'd had a good look round, reckoned there was some top stuff Denny could flog as his usual persona, and Patrick had told him about it. Then Macey had got there first, nicked that necklace, tried to palm it off on Denny, and as he wanted to take over The Cardigan Estate at some point, he'd thought it'd be amusing to steal from The Brothers' shop prior to stealing their status as leaders.

If George and Greg caught up with Denny, would he drop Patrick in the shit or keep quiet? And now Patrick was on their payroll—he clearly didn't have a choice about it—things were even worse. As he was the twins' latest informant, his loyalty had to solely be with them; it should have been before now, what with him paying them protection money to keep his pub safe, yet he'd got involved with The Network anyway.

When The Brothers had spoken to him, all gobby and menacing, Patrick had acted scared of them, but in fact, he was a big bloke, too, and he had a few murders under his belt, so he thought of them as on a par. Still, he'd behaved like he had to throw them off the scent while chucking Denny to the wolves, something he regretted now because it could come back to bite him on the arse.

He paid Nance to deal with the Bassett Hound for the most part, only came here to show his face every so often so he could work for Denny as and when at the refugee house and wherever he was needed. Nance kept it quiet from Liv that Patrick was usually elsewhere, he paid her enough to zip her trap. Patrick's wife didn't need to know the ins and outs, she just liked living off the money the pub generated and wasn't interested in anything else, and the times he worked for Denny, late into the night, well, pub hours were the perfect cover, especially because the discos went on until three in the morning at weekends.

Everyone at the refugee house called him Patrick, and he called them by their names, too, apart from Beaker, who'd refused to say who he really was. He had the right idea, clever kid. For the first time, Patrick disagreed with Denny about something. He should have stuck to what the big boss wanted—all of them calling each other Minion with their assigned number after it. Patrick was Minion-57. He ought to insist on being called that in future, but how could he expect that to happen when Denny was his boss and would likely overrule him?

Fuck it. Why had Patrick bloody come here today when he was supposed to be doing something else? Why had he shown his face? If he *hadn't* been here, he wouldn't have had to speak to the twins.

Shit. If The Brothers went to Beaker's... Patrick had lied when he'd said he thought Beaker's ramblings were bullshit. They were real, Patrick saw what happened on a regular fucking basis.

x

What if Beaker cracked and told them about what he did for Denny, babysitting the women? What if they poked into The Network business? Patrick would get a right rollicking off Denny if he found out George and Greg had been here; they'd said they wouldn't let on it had been him who'd spilt the beans, but you couldn't trust anyone completely, could you. Should Patrick warn him they might be on the snoop?

Patrick would have to be careful. The last thing he needed was the twins turning up at the refugee house and seeing him there, although he always had a disguise on. What if they followed him around, thinking he'd acted dodgy just now when they'd spoken?

He calmed himself down. Because of Patrick's disguise, Beaker wouldn't know he was also the landlord of his local pub. Patrick changed his voice when with people from The Network, gruffer, and he came across as someone totally different. So what if he was called Patrick. There were hundreds of those in London. He racked his brain to think whether Beaker had ever seen him as his pub persona in his SUV, the same one he used to ferry Denny about. There was one time Patrick had seen Beaker going to the flat above the chippy, and that was how he knew he lived there, but he didn't think Beaker had clocked him.

And what about Angie? Fucking hell, Liv would be on the blower shortly, crying her eyes out. The police would have to go round to the in-laws' gaff and break the bad news—*they might have already done it*—then Liv would be told, and he'd have to act all shocked about the murder—as shocked as he'd been when he'd found out from the twins, because shit, he hadn't expected that—plus she'd want him hanging around to comfort her, playing the good husband. How could he get out of doing that? He had an urgent job to do for Denny, one he'd forgone carrying out on his way home last night. A body currently lay in Patrick's boot, and he had to get it to the woods and bury it.

He'd have to do it sooner rather than later. Liv was bound to phone within the hour. Did he have time to dispose of that dead slag? It'd be a rush job, but a rush was better than leaving her in the SUV.

He washed his face, straightened out his features, and returned to the bar. Some bloke had been in all day, all week now Patrick came to

41

think of it. He sipped lemonade, seeming content to soak in the atmosphere and occasionally fiddle about on his phone. Christ, had The Network sent someone to spy? Or was he one of the twins' fellas? Nah, that didn't make sense. Why would George and Greg have ordered him to stand there when they hadn't known about the robbery until today?

Or has he been watching out for Macey?

Stop it, you're being paranoid.

He glanced around, checking for other strangers. While there were some, who ate their grub and chatted as normal, the rest were locals. All seemed well, and he took a deep breath, going up to Nance and giving her the wink that he was off, and if Liv rang, to tell her to reach him on his mobile because he'd be down in the cellar. They both knew he wouldn't be. Nance thought he had another woman, hence his time away from the pub, and while she'd said she didn't agree with aiding and abetting in extra-marital-affair stuff, she'd keep quiet for a price. Cash in hand on top of her already decent wages.

In his office, he slipped on his overalls, a black wig, put gloves over his shaking hands, slid his mobile in his pocket, and left the pub via the back door, switching the plates on the SUV from his to some random numbers and letters. If the body was ever found and the police trawled through CCTV, they'd spot the make and model but wouldn't know it was him driving it. For the purposes of ANPR and photo capture, he slapped on the black beard he always wore when working for Denny, then took the roads least likely to have big brother watching.

In the woods, he parked up behind some thick bushes, aware he or the vehicle might be spotted by dog walkers, considering the time of day. He got out, slung the slag over his shoulder, and walked into the denser area ahead where, if he was lucky, no one else would venture. He dropped her on the ground, recalling how he'd strangled the life out of her, how she'd fought until the bitter end, the other women watching on in horror. He smirked, adjusted his hard-on, and returned to the car, taking out a wide-ended shovel. Usually, he needed about four or five hours to dig a decent enough grave, or he had help from others in The Network which reduced the time, but he didn't have the bloody luxury of that now, did he.

He toiled for half an hour, a shallow grave that was enough for the body to nestle in but could possibly be discovered in the near future. Dogs had a habit of sniffing shit out, digging, and if one of them wasn't trained right and didn't respond to their owner's recall, they could unearth this bitch in no time.

Fucking hell.

He dug for another half an hour, then his phone rang with the unique ringtone for Liv. He could ignore it, he did that often enough and she was used to it, but in the circumstances…

"All right, love?" he asked, all chirpy.

"Oh God, please come home."

"What's the matter? Have you fucked up the computer again?" He laughed, congratulating himself on sounding normal.

"No, it's Angie."

"Aww, don't say she's forgotten the alarm code for the shop. It's five, four—"

"Patrick, shut up. She's *dead*."

"What?" Patrick stared at the slag. *She's dead an' all*. He almost cracked up but stopped himself. "How?"

"Someone robbed the shop. They slit…slit her *throat*!"

"Fuck me sideways, Liv, I'm so sorry…"

"Just get to my mum and dad's. They're in bits."

He choked back laughter again. Normally, he chopped the slags into bits before burying them, but again, he didn't have time today. This one would be dumped intact. "I bet they are. This is bloody awful. Listen, I'm in the cellar, one of the beer pipes has burst and lager's pissed everywhere. I'll be with you as soon as I can, all right?"

"Okay, okay… Oh shit. Okay…"

"Deep breath."

Liv released a strangled screech. "Oh my *God*! Mum! *Mum*? I have to go. She's just collapsed."

The line went as dead as Angie and the slag, and he allowed himself to chortle then, the sounded echoing. He composed himself— someone might have heard him—and kicked the body into the hole. He shovelled mud over her, glancing around for debris to throw on top so it looked like the rest of the forest floor, but twigs and whatnot were sparse here, so he left it as it was and went back to the car.

He took his overalls and footwear off, putting them in the boot, reminding himself he'd have to clean it out in case any evidence had been left behind—or mud from the woods transferred and could link the murder to him. In the driver's seat, he reached into the passenger footwell for his nice shoes and put them on, then removed the beard, wig, and gloves, stuffing them in the compartment on the dash. Hopefully, the mother-in-law's collapse would be serious and she'd have to be taken to hospital, tying Liv up so Patrick had the excuse to leave every so often to say he had to go home and let their German Shepherd out to do his business. He'd have to let Denny know it might be a bit tricky to help him out for a while, but he'd do his best to be at the refugee house or ferrying him around as and when.

Fuck Angie having the gall to get murdered. She'd really fucked things up. And fuck Denny for doing it.

Chapter Four

*T*o have a sister as your best friend was one of the finer things in life. Someone who matched you in thought and deed, who wanted peace in life, to just be happy. Oleksiy and Bohuslava were the same yet not. Oleksiy had more confidence, more faith in having a happy ending in all things, whereas Bohuslava tended to hug caution like it was a lifeline, something to keep her afloat. Steady. She balked at change, resisted it, wanting the safety of what she already knew. No surprises, no spontaneity. Everything had to be mapped out so she was aware of what was coming.

Twelve-year-old Oleksiy didn't mind surprises, the good kind. Mother had arranged one today, and they sat in the garden, food laid out, Father arriving from Kyiv where he worked, back for a week, then he'd be off again for months. Oleksiy hadn't been expecting him, so to see him appear as they'd been setting the buffet meal out had been a welcome shock, the happiest. Bohuslava, though, she'd stood there taking it all in, as if her mind couldn't process it, and her scowl said: Why wasn't I told about this? She'd directed her angry expression at Mother who'd ignored it, rushing up to her husband, the love of her life.

Gifts were presented by Father, as always. Jewellery, pretty sandals, lovely dresses.

"Things for my princesses," he said.

"You overindulge them," Mother admonished, ever mindful of the plight of her people, how so many had struggled in the past, gifts like these only dreams for the poor, nothing to be owned in their lifetimes.

Yet she held her new dress up and paraded around on the grass, asking if it suited her.

"Of course it does," Father said. "Otherwise, why would I have bought it?"

She slipped her feet into her high-heeled sandals—
"Where would I ever go to wear these?"—and pranced
around, secretly enjoying the extravagance, Oleksiy
thought, despite her dogged determination for them
never to become like their president, someone who
craved expensive things and purportedly got them via
corruption.

"You'll wear them tomorrow night at a dance,"
Father said, "with the dress."

"But what about the children?"

"The sitter will come."

Oleksiy loved the sitter, Old Yana, who let them
stay up late and watch TV. She brought sweets and ice
cream, popcorn, and only shooed them to bed when
Father's headlights lit up the living room curtains.

"Quickly, quickly," she'd say. "Eyes shut, pretend
to be asleep when they come in and kiss you!"

Oleksiy rubbed the material of her dress between
finger and thumb. It wasn't real silk, Mother would
never allow that, but it looked the same. She longed to
put it on, to feel like royalty, but Mother whisked it
away and draped it over the top of the open back door,
then scooped up Bohuslava's and did the same, adding
her own last.

"We'll go somewhere special for you to wear them,"
she said, "and I don't want them to get dirty."

Bohuslava had calmed down now, crawled out of her self-constructed shell, and sat on Father's lap, listening to his stories, as they always did, about his time away. Much laughter, so much happiness it was hard for Bohuslava to stay cross about the surprise of his homecoming for long.

"When are you going back?" she asked.

Father reared his head back, feigning hurt, a hand to his chest. "I've only just got here. Do you want to get rid of me so soon?"

"I need to know."

So he told her, and she relaxed, likely filing the information away so she could prepare herself for him leaving. The upset. The tears. The asking why he had to stay away for so long when he only worked in Kyiv. Then Mother and Father would look at each other in that secret way they had, and Oleksiy would once again suspect he didn't work in Kyiv at all but somewhere else, too far away for him to return often.

Bohuslava hugged him around the neck, possibly because she'd already been imagining the day he'd leave. She was ten years old and had never 'fitted inside herself' as Mother had put it, the odd duck, the one who wasn't like anyone else in the family, the one who wasn't comfortable with who she was. Gangly *legs too long for her body, a colt, Father called her, all skittish and unsure.*

"Why can't you be more like Oleksiy?" they'd said.

"Because I'm not Oleksiy," she'd said. "I'm me."

Which was true, and Oleksiy loved her for standing firm in who she was. Why try to change her? She wouldn't be Bohuslava if they did, she'd be someone else, and that would be weird.

They ate, Mother and Father drank, and music played, Father grabbing their hands to encourage them to dance—Oleksiy going with him immediately, Bohuslava's scowl coming back until she decided she could join them.

The summer sun beamed down well into the evening, Mother and Father merry drunk, their faces flushed with love. It was safe here, with them, and Oleksiy didn't want to be anywhere else. She wished Father didn't have to work away and they could be like this all the time and said so.

"It's because *he works away that him coming home is like this," Mother said. "One big party. If he was here all the time... Could we put up with his stinky feet* every *day?"*

"Hey," Father said, smiling.

Then he chuckled, threatened to take his boots off, and everyone else screamed for him to keep them on.

Life was good even when he wasn't there, Mother their saviour, so kind, so free with her hugs. She worked hard in a factory, fed them, picked out pretty clothes, and on Saturdays they went to the market, where she shepherded them to the ice cream shop afterwards and they filled their bellies until they felt sick.

Compared to some, they were privileged.

No, Oleksiy never wanted to leave this idyllic world her parents had created for them, even though it was tainted by the things certain men in governments did and said. The word 'war' seemed to have always been there, so much so it was the same as 'life', because to live here with the humming threat in the background was life, it was all they knew.

They just had to make the best of it while they could, that was all. To think of the future, where it could all go so wrong, was to invite doom, Father had said. What you put out into the universe came back to you, so if you predicted war, you'd get war, and if you predicted peace, you'd receive it. But there was proof that even if you predicted war you could still live in peace, because wasn't that what they were doing now? Mother, Oleksiy, and Bohuslava knew things wouldn't stay this way forever, an attack would come eventually, but they still had a good life, they were richer than many and should be grateful for it. They had food on the table, the bills paid. Yes, they had to save for some things, but it wasn't anything like it had been for Mother and Father growing up.

Mother had said the universe speech was his way of calming their fears, that he wasn't a silly man who believed they'd be safe just because he wanted it to be so.

Now, she swayed as she drank. "Your father does his best to give you good memories. You're children, and childhood should be a happy time, not like it was for us, so when he's not here and we're sad about it, we'll go to Kyiv for the weekend."

Bohuslava opened her mouth to protest at yet another surprise being sprung.

Mother smiled. "You can wear your dress, your sandals, and we'll have syriniki…"

Bohuslava's favourite curd pancakes with sugar on top, and fruit sauce, which might convince her.

The rest of what Mother said faded into the background with Oleksiy viewing the city in her mind, such a big place, so many things to see and do. They'd go to St Sophia Cathedral; Mother always paid it a visit while there. It was topped with what Oleksiy thought of as sage-green hats on the turrets, and on top of that, golden balls, crosses reaching for the sky.

Inside, Mother would delight at the vastness of it, the beauty, and light a candle for Father to keep him safe when he was away from home.

They'd stroll through Maidan Nezalezhnosti (Independence Square) in Khreshchatyk Street. If they walked there in the evening, there'd be music, people enjoying themselves.

Then there was the inevitable gawp at Mezhyhirya, the home of the president. The last time they'd been, Mother had tutted at the display of extravagance. She never failed to take them there, to show them how the president lived in splendour while the rest of the country tried to feed itself.

"Institutional greed and corruption," she'd said.

It boasted an equestrian club, a shooting range, a helicopter pad, tennis courts, hunting grounds, and the most overindulgence of all, a private zoo.

"Never forget what it's like," Mother usually said. "He fills his face with pies while people go hungry. He spends money like water while others scrabble to find coins. Always help those who need it. If you can hold out your hand to stop someone from drowning, do it, for he doesn't, and many suffer because of him."

Oleksiy loved to admire the opulence, to imagine being a princess, yet Mother's words drew her out of her fantasy and heaped guilt on her. If Mezhyhirya's *copper roof represented tyranny and selfishness, if living somewhere so rich when others lived on the street… She kept her imaginings to herself.*

"So you wait to have the fun when I'm gone?" Father pretended to sound hurt. "You would leave me out?"

"Why on earth would you want to come to Kyiv with us when you spend all your working life there?" That look again from Mother.

Bohuslava laughed. It was good to see her happy, to be comfortable now the initial shock of Father coming home had subsided. What must it be like to live in her head? To constantly need to know what was coming at her? To not trust, to be wary? Oleksiy felt she needed to look after her sister, to protect her, to be her advocate, her safety blanket. She would be, even when they were grown up. If ever they were in danger, Oleksiy would get them out of it.

If ever Bohuslava needed her, she'd be there.
Always.

Chapter Five

Beaker shouted obscenities into his headset. God, some people on Xbox were right twats. They acted tough, making out they were someone to be reckoned with, but he had a feeling they were weedy lads who only had balls when they hid behind their TV screens. He was a bit like that himself so recognised it in others.

Agreeing to work for Denny had been a genius move on Beaker's part. He had loads of money now—or loads to him anyway—and he was protected by being an employee. If he needed someone dealt with, he told Denny their name, and the boss scared them off. Denny likened himself to The Brothers, although privately, Beaker thought he was nothing like them. They were right hard bastards, rumoured to torture people if they put a foot wrong, whereas Denny was more the mouthy variety, using his words to threaten, to frighten.

Beaker opted out of the game, took his headset off, and went into the kitchen for a can of Coke. A *can*. He could afford those now, and the real brand, not the two-litre bottles of fake stuff from Aldi. He was coming up in the world, even ate Walkers now, and his bills were always paid on time.

He looked after the girls, those refugees, at a house on the edge of Cardigan where a speck of countryside separated it from Moon's estate. Beaker got a taxi there every evening, staying over until eight in the morning. Once he was home, he got some kip, then in the afternoons he played Xbox, had a bit of grub, and off he went to work, which wasn't work, not really. He fucked about on his phone most of the time, a glorified babysitter, and sometimes, if the refugees woke up and banged on the floor, as instructed, he unlocked their door and took them to the loo, gave them water.

The wages kept him doing as he was told, but it was wrong, what he did. What Denny and the others did. The Network had some right rum people in it, men who'd cut your knackers off without a smidgen of guilt, so Denny had said. Beaker quite liked his knackers so obeyed instructions, but he still thought locking people up then sending them off to have sex with people was rotten.

He'd mentioned it to the landlord at the Bassett Hound once, wanting to gauge Patrick's reaction, see if buying refugees was as bad as Beaker thought. Patrick had laughed, though, said he was full of it, and that Beaker was lucky he'd only said that to Patrick, because if he'd told anyone else and Denny found out…

Lesson learnt. Beaker hadn't spoken about it to anyone outside The Network since, and he'd worried for ages that Patrick would tell Denny what he'd said. Seemed Patrick really had thought he was joking, because Denny was the same as always with Beaker. If he knew he'd breathed a word about The Network, surely he'd have got someone to shut him up for good.

He popped the tab on the can and took a long swig. Thought about what to have for dinner. Most evenings he nipped downstairs to the chippy, pure laziness, plus he wasn't a good cook, but today he fancied a Chinese. He ordered it on Uber Eats, busying himself by taking the washing out of the machine and stuffing it in the tumble dryer. He could afford the electric these days, so no more hanging it on an airer or the rads.

The doorbell dinged, and he frowned. Surely his dinner wasn't here already, was it? The Chinese place was quick, but bloody hell...

He prodded the ON button of the dryer and walked down the hallway, peering through the peephole. Two men stood on the balcony, and he didn't need an introduction. What the fuck were *they* doing here? Legs going weak, he contemplated ignoring them, but his food would come, and if they hung around in the street, they'd see him at the door.

Shit.

He opened up. "Oh. All right?" Casual was best.

It seemed one of the twins didn't think so. A shove to Beaker's chest had him sprawling backwards, banging into the wall and stubbing his toe on the skirting board. His chest tightened, his mouth dried, and he righted himself as they entered and closed the door. The hallway wasn't big enough for those two, the walls seemed to close in, and Beaker reversed towards the living room doorway, pointing to it to let them know where he was going, because words had failed him.

He sat on the sofa, trying to act calm, arms spread along the back of it. Sweat sprouted in his pits, the scent of fear pungent, so he put his arms by his sides. The Brothers came in, one blocking the doorway.

The other went to the window and looked down at the street. He turned from his perusal and smiled at Beaker. "I'm George, just in case you were wondering who's who. We'd like a word with you. There's a little job we need doing, and we've decided you're the one to do it. If it gets us what we want, we'll give you five grand."

"Y-you what?" Beaker couldn't believe it. Five grand? "Um, I'm not into hurting anybody…"

"It's nothing like that." George smiled again. "Let's call it watching and listening, then telling us where a certain person is going to be at a certain time."

"What person?" Although he knew. It had to be Denny, didn't it?

"Before I reveal that, let's go over the consequences should you feel the need to tell our target what's going on."

Beaker swallowed. Wished he had his Coke in here. His throat was well parched. "O-okay."

"We've got this rack. Nice little number. Metal, attached to a wall. It's got spikes on it, so when you're trussed up there, manacles holding you in a star shape, if you're not careful, the spikes dig into you. In your case, if you end up there, I reckon I'll make this handy thing to ensure the spikes poke right through your back and into your body. It'll have a long handle, and on the end, a square of wood. I'll run at you, whack the square onto your gut, and it'll push you backwards onto the spikes. I suspect the points will pop out the front and embed in the square, but that's okay, I can wrench it off. That'll hurt. A lot. After that, I'll get you down, lay you out on the floor, and while you're still alive, I'll cut you up with my circular saw. Into two-inch slices."

The description had transferred into Beaker's head as a vivid scene, one where blood dripped and he screamed, begging George to stop. His brain added nasty laughter, the twins roaring with it, patting each other on the back on a job well done. He thought of Nan and how she'd wonder where he was when he didn't go round for dinner on Sundays, how she'd report him missing and get hold of Beaker's mum, even though he had nothing to do with her anymore. The police would try to find him, but Beaker would be long gone.

"I'll do whatever you want, I-I swear."

George grinned. "I thought you might. Now then, this is what's going to happen…"

Beaker listened to it all. Yes, he could do that. Watch, listen, pass on some information. But how had they found out he worked for Denny? He'd do what George had suggested and make sure other people were around when Denny announced where he'd be going, whenever, so Beaker wasn't the only one suspected of being a grass, although what did it matter if Denny was going to be killed?

The Network. They might come after me, so it does *matter.*

If Beaker did well, the twins said they'd employ him as a snitch once the heat had died down after Denny had been apprehended. He thought of the five grand. That was enough to get him by until they took him on permanently. The social paid the rent and council tax, and so long as he went to interviews set up for him, he'd get his benefits. Lucky for him, he was classed as a thicko, and no one ever offered him a proper job because he acted dim as fuck. He knew how to game the system. He'd learnt from the best: his druggy mother.

"I notice you haven't denied knowledge about the refugees," George said.

"It's wrong, that's what it is, but I just babysit. I don't have anything to do with the nasty stuff."

"Nasty stuff?"

"You know, driving them to the people who have sex with them and shit."

"What I want to know is, why you've never come and told us about this before now. I assume it's all happening on our patch."

Beaker nodded. "Yeah, it does, on the edge of Cardigan, close to Moon's. There's a house there, behind a load of trees. It's a shithole, to be honest. It used to belong to some farmer or other."

"You didn't answer my question."

Beaker scanned his brain to recall what it had been. "Oh. Yeah. I didn't tell you cos Denny said if I did, he'd kill me."

George laughed. "Did he now."

"He threatens all of us. Said he'd duff up my nan, knows where she lives."

Greg propped himself up on the wall beside the door. "That's pissed me off."

George looked at him. "Shall we send her on a little holiday, just in case?"

Beaker's guts went south. "What sort of holiday? What do you mean?"

George ignored him and said to Greg, "Deal with it."

Greg wandered into the hallway, and the front door opened then shut.

Beaker panicked. "You won't hurt her, will you?"

George scowled at him. "Nah. We know a bloke who knows a bloke, and there's this chalet in Southend. Nan can go there for the week. We'll give you the money for her train fare and any food she needs once she's settled in. Make out you paid for it, that you want her to have a nice break. You'll nip round to hers before you go to that refugee house, get her on the train, see her off. She can collect the keys from the reception hut there."

"But she's got work."

"Where?"

"At the bingo hall. Bullingdon's."

George smiled. "We'll pay the manager a visit. We know her. She'll be made to understand your nan can take a week off."

Beaker relaxed. Nan would love a holiday. She'd been going on about one since Grandad had died. She'd be out of the way, and Denny wouldn't be able to get to her. "All right. Okay."

"What can you tell me about Macey Moorhouse?"

Beaker had to think about that. "I haven't seen her for a while, not since she punched that woman at the pub disco."

"The one at Bassett Hound?"

"Yeah. She was off her head, face full of makeup—I say that because her lipstick was all smeared and it stuck in my mind."

"She stole from us today. Robbed our shop. She was there when our manager got her throat sliced."

"Fucking hell. I know she's nicks stuff and sells it on, but I didn't know she was into that kind of shit."

"If you hear anything, let us know."

Greg came back in carrying a white bag. "Chinese? I took it off the delivery bloke while I was outside on the phone."

"You'd best eat it quick," George said. "You've got a lot to get done before you go to work."

Beaker got up and took the bag from Greg. He wasn't that hungry now, but if he didn't eat, he went all squiffy. Nan said it was something to do with dipping sugar levels.

Greg patted Beaker's shoulder. "We're in luck. The chalet's free."

George nodded. "We'd have found her somewhere else if it wasn't." He looked at Beaker. "Don't just stand there! Chop-chop, son."

Chapter Six

Macey sat in the meeting room, pissed off she'd been living here for just over a week. She'd been rude to Denny on the phone, apparently, and he'd taken exception to it, and now he dictated what she did. She couldn't believe she'd stepped into his trap.

She'd been in Bumble's Café last week, ringing him about the necklace she'd nicked from

Vintage Finds. It had been in the glass counter, and she'd got the manager to take it out so she could have a closer look at it. Of course, she'd had a wig on and a ton of makeup, but she'd still worried Angie had known it was her. Whether she had or hadn't, Macey had legged it out of the shop anyway, a rush of endorphins sending her down the street to an alley, which she'd run down, then she'd got in her car parked nearby.

She'd always stolen from as far back as she could remember. It had started with sweets, small stuff from the corner shop, then progressed to lipstick, mascara, shit like that as a teen, moving to clothes and whatever took her fancy once she'd hit adulthood. She sold it on at half the price and made an okay living.

Taking the necklace had been her first step into the big arena, where she'd get a wedge of cash instead of pin money to tide her over until the next theft. She'd phoned Denny, asked for a grand, told him it was worth twice that—and that it was hot. What she hadn't told him at that point was where she'd stolen it from. If he'd known it was The Brothers' shop right from the off, he might not have been interested. Even Denny wasn't stupid enough to tangle with them. Yet

Macey had. She'd thrown caution to the wind, the devil on her shoulder pushing her to do it.

She must have been off her rocker.

She'd sent Denny a message once she'd got home after that bloke had robbed her in broad daylight—whoever it was had used Denny's car. She'd demanded he give the necklace back. All she'd received in return was a line of laughter emojis, then a second text saying: MEET ME ON THE CORNER OF SMITH STREET, TONIGHT, 7 P.M. She'd gone, of course she had, and even though she'd known it had the potential to turn nasty, there she'd been, waiting for his blue sports car. Instead, he'd turned up in a black SUV, one she hadn't seen before. She'd got inside the back, and he'd sat there, smirking.

The car pulled off, the driver some thug-like bearded fella who kept glancing at Macey in the rearview mirror. Uncomfortable, she stared into the footwell at her shoes, flat ones in case she had to run once they got to their destination.

"I want you to work for me," Denny said.

She whipped her head to face him, shocked by what he'd said. "You want me to nick for you?"

"Not the shit you usually pinch, no. Bigger stuff."

She wasn't sure she wanted to be governed by a wannabe Brother. Denny was scary, yes, he had a way with words that had people shitting themselves, but the idea of having to answer to him, to steal on spec... It wasn't her thing. She was a lone wolf, always had been, and she didn't want to change that. Although she was *curious. If she could get him to open up, she'd then have something on him. She could use that to get him to leave her alone.*

"What sort of stuff?" she asked.

"Shit from jewellers' shops. Rings and watches from people's homes. There are a few I know who have Rolexes and whatever."

"I don't do breaking and entering."

"You should. It's lucrative."

She shook her head. "It's too risky. The world and his wife have cameras these days. Alarms."

"No different to shops."

"I rob those in the daytime and know how to avoid cameras, know what to do to the tags to stop the alarms going off. The sort you're talking about, they're different, and you know it."

"Someone would be with you to deal with it."

She didn't like the sound of that. Too many cooks spoiled the broth. "What sort of someone?"

"The person who nicked the necklace off you for me."

"Right…"

"Are you in or not?"

"Depends what places we're hitting. I like to know where I'm going in advance so I can plan accordingly."

"The plans have already been made, so you don't need to worry about those, and I'll let you in on the first job so you can think about it. You've been there before, so it shouldn't faze you. Vintage Finds."

She laughed. Was he off his head on coke or something? "I've not long robbed it, and I need to lie low. Do you seriously think it's a good idea to go back? When I went there, only one camera was behind the counter. I assume the twins hadn't got around to having more installed, or, more likely, they're so up their own arses, they thought no one would dare to rob them."

"That's the beauty of going back again. They've got loads of cameras now, had them installed this afternoon, and we'll be getting the message across that despite that, despite who they are, I'm ballsy enough to play with them. They've been sending men out to ask about you and—"

Her fear spiked. "What?"

73

"Oh, didn't you know that? It's only been a few hours, and already they're on the hunt. They know it was you. I'm surprised no one's been round your gaff to pick you up."

Her stomach rolled over. Fucking hell, she'd have sworn she'd covered all bases. It must have been Angie. "How?"

"Don't ask me. No clue, although I suspect the woman who manages it tipped them off. Did you wear a mask?"

"No I fucking didn't! I'm not Zorro."

"You will be."

"Pardon?"

"Nothing." He stared out of the window at the countryside passing by.

Where were they going? Or was this little trip just so they could chat without anyone except the driver listening? A good move on Denny's part because he could deny the conversation had even taken place if she went to The Brothers and spilled the beans. That was a thought. She could make out Denny had forced her to steal from Vintage in the first place, that she'd been so scared of him she'd done whatever he'd asked.

He turned back to her. "Are you in?"

"Only if you give me that grand for the necklace. I needed that cash to pay my rent." She wasn't in, she just wanted the dosh, but he didn't need to know that.

He chuckled, dipped a hand in his suit, and she stiffened, worried he'd bring out a gun. She imagined him shooting her in the face, point blank range, her brains smacking into the side window.

He handed her an envelope. "Exactly what I thought you'd say. You're in now, you've taken the money. No backing out."

Fuck. She hadn't been thinking straight. She should have known he'd snag her when her mind had been on the grand. That was how Denny worked, underhand, sneaky. She knew this, so why hadn't she been more careful?

"When's the job?" she asked.

"Next week. You'll get the details in a bit when we get to where we're going. Where you'll be living for a while. I can't have you going home and the twins collecting you. There's something else I want you to do for me in the meantime. Two hundred quid an evening. There's some tarts I need you to put makeup on. They haven't got the foggiest how to do it properly, and I've seen you about when you've got your slap on, and you're good at it."

She didn't wear makeup if she wasn't out and about. Well, not the amount she caked on for jobs or going to the pub anyway. Without it, she was just a nondescript woman who could go about her life spending the money from the spoils. With it, she didn't look like herself, so if a still of her face from a CCTV capture was ever put on the news, no one would take a blind bit of notice of her when she was bare-faced.

"Why do I need to put makeup on people, and who are they?"

Denny grinned. "That, Little Thief, is something you'll find out in about five minutes."

She wished she'd never been told. Never been shown the women on mattresses in the big house. Some of them had been here for a while, it was obvious by the way they acted, how they didn't huddle in on themselves and presented a hardened front, but the new ones, fucking hell, Macey didn't like seeing those. She hated what they represented — people who shouldn't even be here, living in the UK. They belonged in their own countries.

From what she'd gathered by listening, a company called The Network had a system where all new recruits were brought to the house and taught how to behave, what to do with clients, in the biggest bedroom that had a plaque on the door with ONE etched into it. A few of Denny's men gave them a taste of what was to come, and Macey swore they were rough on purpose. She knew they didn't treat the women nicely by the screams and cries coming from upstairs, and the first time she'd heard them, she'd made a move to leave, get the fuck out of there, but the driver of the SUV had told her to sit down and shut the fuck up if she knew what was good for her.

Of course, she'd sat, shitting herself, grateful it wasn't her going through that ordeal. Afterwards, when the newbies had been allowed to shower, Macey had done their makeup, and some other woman styled their hair. June, she was called, and Macey recognised her from the salon in town, although June didn't seem to know who Macey was.

That was the thing with people, wasn't it. Everyone presented themselves to the world as whatever they wanted others to think they were, but some harboured dark secrets. There was Macey with her theft tricks, June with her moonlighting job at the house, and no one would guess they did such tacky shit behind the scenes. That was probably just as well, because if they *did* know, then they'd be aware Denny pulled the strings, and if *that* got out, God help them.

Macey stared over at SUV Man, Patrick. His thick black hair and beard had him appearing thuggish, but his eyes were like that twat's from the Bassett Hound, the landlord. Bright blue, same shape. He didn't sound or look like him, though, so she must be being fanciful. Mind you, she was always drunk by the time she got to that pub on her weekly benders.

He picked meat out of his teeth with a fingernail. Denny provided a takeaway dinner each night, so at least Macey didn't have to fork out for that, but she hated eating food she thought of as tainted. Tainted by what went on here. The air was thick with the smell of *wrongness*—she couldn't describe it any other way—and every breath she took threatened to choke her.

She shifted her attention to Denny who sat at the head of the table like some kind of Mafia don, the twazzock. He had a long way to go before he reached that status, but then again, The Network had trusted him to run this 'branch', so maybe they'd seen something in him that Macey had failed to spot. All she saw was the other Denny, the one who came off as a bit of a prat selling gear from his car boot and banged on about giving to charity, an almost desperate attempt to get people to think of him as a good man. Robin Hood. There was the other side to him, the one he adopted for his dodgy dealings, but never in a million years would she have suspected him of being involved in something so disgusting. Maybe those two personas were an act, to throw people off. Maybe he really did have the balls to give The Brothers a run for their money.

The other person present was Honda, apparently because he'd never buy any other brand of motorbike. Well, what else could she call him but a murderer? When she'd seen Angie dead because he'd slit her throat, she'd crapped herself. She was in deeper than she'd ever wanted to be. She'd thought the shotgun had been a prop to get Angie to open the counter, or to threaten whoever had come into the shop via the back, that they'd take the jewellery, leave, and not look back. Except Honda had other ideas. If only Angie hadn't tried to press that alarm button. Honda had got shitty, and the rest was history.

"Someone say something, for fuck's sake," she said, desperate to know the score about the robbery. "Why was Angie killed? Why wasn't I told about that before going in?"

Denny smiled. "Because I needed some insurance. You're an accessory to murder now, and it ensures you'll keep your trap shut and do what I want, no question."

"You bastard!" she blurted.

"Oh, I'm the biggest one out there, darlin'." He leant back and splayed his fingers on the table. "And I'll let it slide, what you just called me. This time. Let me give you a little lesson in learning to read people. Look beyond what they show you. Never take anyone at face value. I mean, you thought I was just a wheeler and dealer, didn't you. It's okay, you can admit it."

She nodded.

"Yet here we are." He gestured to the room. "You and me, we're alike. You present a façade to the world with your makeup, just like I pretend I'm a wheeler-dealer who's possibly a bit thick on the uptake and likes helping charities. In reality, I'm more than that. I've been working behind the scenes, and The Brothers have no clue that I'm anyone but what I want them to see. This is how you get ahead in life, Macey. You play the long game. You work quietly and diligently until it's time to make your move."

"And what move's that?"

He gave her a sly look. "I'm taking The Cardigan Estate."

She spluttered out laughter, couldn't help herself.

"Didn't you hear what I just said?" Denny asked. "Clearly not, because otherwise, you wouldn't be laughing. You're thinking of the Denny everyone *thinks* they know, the one I wanted them to know. *He* couldn't possibly take the estate, I'll give you that. But what you need to get into your thick little head is *that* Denny isn't real. The one who buys refugees and makes money off them is. The one who sends people like you out to become involved in murder is." He paused, glaring at her. "Don't underestimate me, Little Thief. It'll be your downfall."

She hated him calling her that.

Macey swallowed, needing a drink of water. She reached for the glass in front of her, the ice long melted. She drank, her mind whirling with what he'd said. She was in a mess whichever way she looked at it. The Brothers were already after her for the necklace, and if they viewed the CCTV at Vintage from today and somehow recognised her, even with that stupid Zorro mask Denny had forced her to put on, she'd be dead if they got hold of her.

And dead if she didn't do what Denny wanted.

I'm so fucked.

Chapter Seven

*F*ather had died on a sunny day while sitting in his deckchair in the garden. His heart, so the doctor had said, and, "Thank goodness he was here, with you, and not in Kyiv with people who don't love him as much."

A platitude that was meant to soothe but had given sixteen-year-old Bohuslava the horrors. Of course, as Oleksiy had known her sister would, she'd then entertained him dying either alone or in front of his work colleagues, how it would have been a case of them wanting the body out of his office as soon as possible, the shock of it all turning people in on themselves instead of reaching out to touch his hand, going slowly cold, to grasp it as Mother had, to send him on his way knowing he'd been loved.

Oleksiy had tried to stop Bohuslava from going down that route, tormenting herself with what could have been, and urging her to concentrate on what was—Father had died at home, his wife and girls close by, in his sleep, peaceful, as if God had sucked his soul away gently, no fuss, no pain. He'd deserved a death like that, as he'd been a good man, kind and generous. Funny.

He'd be missed.

Mother hadn't realised he'd gone to begin with, none of them had. One second Father had been snoring, then he hadn't. Mother had joked she'd best check to see if he was still breathing, because: "The man snores all the time, never a quiet moment."

The shock of discovering he wasn't *breathing…*

Old Yana had come, to cook, to clean, to do everything Mother did while she grieved and mourned to such a degree, Oleksiy and Bohuslava hadn't seen her for days. She kept to her bedroom, her pitiful wails floating through the door and filling the house.

"It will pass," Yana had said. "She will love again."

"No." Oleksiy had shaken her head. "She will never be with anyone else. He was her soul mate."

"Then this will get better, for her and for you. Grief never goes away, it lives inside us, choosing to come out when you least expect it, but she will function again, she will laugh." Yana had rocked in Father's wooden chair. "To begin with, the very thought of the dead hurts, but in time, instead of being broken inside when their faces or words enter your head, you learn to smile at them, for those memories keep them alive, never to be forgotten. Think of the good times. Smile, for your father wouldn't want you all to be so unhappy."

"He didn't work in Kyiv, did he," Oleksiy had blurted. "He lied to us, she lied to us. If he lived there, he'd have been home more often."

"It's not for me to say," Yana had said, "but know that wherever he went, it was for all of you."

"So they kept a secret from us?" Bohuslava had sniffled. "Why?"

Yana had rocked harder. "Some people have jobs they're not allowed to discuss. It wasn't a secret, more an order. Leave it at that, eh?"

Oleksiy scrunched her eyes closed. She didn't want to think about it. Instead, she'd live her life by her father's teachings: what you put out in the universe comes back to you. She'd done her crying and would move forward, thinking only of the good times, keep him alive by laughing at the memories of him, smiling, and who knew, he might be right. If she only radiated happiness, it would come back to her.

Bohuslava, on the other hand, worried that Mother would die the same way, or worse, she'd be knocked down by a speeding car, shot while at the market, strangled at work—or the ultimate scary situation, Father had worked for the government, he knew secrets, and he'd really been killed by the Russians. Bohuslava's mind was a place filled with the remnants of night terrors that lived inside her as if real, as if they were portents that would come true and she just waited for it to happen.

A depressive personality? She always had been one to see the dark side of everything. It was clever to be cautious, she'd said. And if you never hoped for the bright side, you wouldn't be disappointed when your dreams didn't come true. Oleksiy preferred the opposite. She'd dream, she'd wish, she'd encourage the universe to spirit them away from here somehow, if the threat of an invasion became reality.

Fate was a helper, Father had said, if only you asked it to guide you.

What had he put out into the universe in order for it to repay him with death, though?

Maybe they'd never know.

Chapter Eight

In the safe house, her kids in bed, Zoe rested on the sofa opposite Will who sat in an armchair, a coffee table between them. It was a lovely place, such a shame no one lived in it permanently. It seemed a waste, the furniture posh, expensive, the flooring real wood that had been varnished and buffed to a shine. The house could feature in a magazine it was that nice, all hues of grey and white. She could do with living here, wherever it was—she didn't have a clue as she and her boys had been blindfolded on the way. Her sons hadn't minded, thought it was all a bit of a lark and exciting, but it had unnerved her. She trusted the twins, but a tiny voice had whispered: *What if they're getting rid of us?* She'd shaken out of that pretty quickly once Will had chatted ten to the dozen, putting her at ease.

She studied him. He was a nice bloke, sounded like he came from Birmingham, or was that Manchester? She'd never been any good with accents. Anyway, he wasn't from around here, and she found him intriguing. What was someone like him doing working for the twins? What was his backstory? He didn't look mean. People could say the same about her, she supposed. You didn't have to be a thug to work for them, she certainly wasn't. Did Will do any dirty work—as in, get involved with murder? Did she want to know? Really? Yes. If anyone discovered where she was, she needed someone who was willing to protect her sons.

The twins wouldn't have picked him if he wasn't capable.

"Why do you work for them?" she asked.

Will shrugged. "They were good to me once. Too good. I owe them. I don't want to go into it, though. The past is better off staying there. It only torments you if you allow it into the present."

True. *She* allowed the past to poke into the now. How could she not, though? Pete was still in her life because of the kids, and while she couldn't stand the cheating, lying bastard, she didn't want to stop their sons from seeing him. If she could supervise the visits, she would, but they were so much older now and could walk away from him if they didn't like what he said or did. Plus, they'd gathered for themselves what he was really like. Zoe's mum had told her not to influence the boys about Pete, that they'd cotton on to who he was eventually, and she'd been right. She reckoned they only went to see him these days because they got a McDonald's out of it, maybe a few quid pocket money if Pete was feeling generous. Who knew, now he had that new bird—who was closer to their sons' age than his own; what a pervert—Genevieve might put her oar in and suggest he didn't see them anymore. She was bound to want babies of her own and might not like teenagers messing up her life.

Zoe flung the past where it belonged and asked Will, "Do you like what you do?"

"For the most part. What about you?"

She told him her story. "And with two kids to feed, you take what you can get. It just so happens they pay extremely well. All right, I spend a lot of time on my feet, traipsing round after people in my various disguises, but it beats working in the clothes shop. Who wouldn't want to pretend to be a detective every day?"

"Err, I wouldn't, but each to their own."

She laughed at his expression. "Hmm, you don't look like a Poirot or Columbo, I'll give you that. Do you think they'll figure everything out, the twins? You know, put a stop to whatever's going on with Denny and Macey?"

"Yep, without a doubt. They don't stop until they have what they want. Even if it takes months, years, they'll sort it. Not that it ever takes them that long. I'm surprised they haven't found Macey sooner, though. With all the ears on the streets, they normally pull people in pretty quickly. She must have gone into hiding."

"She was such a cocky cow in the café. I hope they take her down a peg. Downright rude to me, she was. Mind you, I was just as cocky. Probably because I have The Brothers behind me, you know, they've got my back so I can afford to be brave in what I say."

"They do tend to give you the feeling of being protected, don't they. Solid blokes, they are. Better than family."

She didn't press him on that. If he'd wanted to elaborate, he would have, but she'd spotted the pain in his eyes at the mention of family.

"Want to play a board game?" he asked, probably a diversion tactic.

She nodded, glancing to a bookshelf with different boxes on it. "Is this place somewhere they hide people on the regular? There's all those books, the games…"

"Yeah. That's why you and your boys were blindfolded on the way. Best you don't know where it is."

"In case I defect and pass info to their enemies?" She smiled. "No chance of me doing that, I won't bite the hands that feed me, but I get why they insisted on it." She paused. "Monopoly?"

He shook his head. "That's shit with two people, and besides, I'm crap at it. What about Dobble?"

"What the hell's *that*?"

"See that little tin there?" He pointed. "It's like Snap but not. Bloody good laugh. Me, Martin, and the twins played it at Christmas while legless."

"You went to them for Christmas?"

"Yeah. They've taken us on as their little brothers."

She got up to collect the tin and sat, opening it to read the instructions. "Ah right. Yep, this will be fun."

She left him to deal the cards out, thinking about what her next job for the twins would be and whether she could continue being on their books if it meant regularly being locked up in a safe house. That couldn't be good for her sons, could it? Although, they'd been happy to use the PlayStation ever since they'd arrived, and the cupboard full of snacks had kept them happy. She'd let them indulge more than she would at home.

Was it too dangerous, this job? What if she got killed? That would mean Pete would get full control of their sons. She shuddered at the thought, and to stop herself from fretting about it,

94

turned her attention to Will and Dobble, determined to beat him.

Chapter Nine

From the spacious balcony of his bedroom, in his large home perched on a cliff, Teo de Luca sat on a rattan chair and stared at the horizon. The sea, a beautiful turquoise, blended with the blue sky, not a cloud in sight. The still-blazing sun, steadily lowering, gilded the water. He was lucky here in Italy. The weather was usually always perfect in the summer, and as he lived alone, he caught an all-over tan, thinking nothing of lying on one of the sunbeds in the nude. He'd thought about having a constant bodyguard—he should, he knew that—but he was so confident in his abilities now to hear an intruder if they got in, he wasn't worried. Once, he hadn't heard a man creeping through the house, and it had fatal consequences, so he'd taught himself to wake at the slightest sound, to nap rather than have a deep sleep.

He didn't want to end up like Papà. Unlike his dear father, he didn't have any family to leave the business and fortune to. His will was made out to various charities in the region, and he'd prepaid for a bronze statue to be built of himself, which the mayor had agreed to put in the market square after his death as a tribute to all he'd done for the locals. As for The Network, he was still undecided who would take it over. No one had shown enough promise yet. Time would tell.

Italy was his main home, the place where he'd been brought up, and if he ever had to leave, he'd miss it. Miss the opulence, the richness of his surroundings, how everyone treated him like royalty, thinking he was a star, a businessman who dealt in antiques, the same lie his father had told. They thought Teo was kind, benevolent, giving to local charities and strengthening the town's economy with handouts. Like Papà had, he held Christmas parties to raise funds for the poor and provide presents for those in need.

No one would believe he was a monster.

A soft breeze blew, and in his peripheral, the sheer curtains billowed into the bedroom, for a moment sending him on high alert, his brain whispering that it wasn't the curtains but a man dressed in white, intent on killing him. He always had that fear now, and was it any wonder? Papà had been murdered by the father of a refugee. Wojciech, an angry Polish man who'd somehow gained information about The Network, had traced it back to Papà. New measures had been put in place so that would never happen again, and so far, the seedy business continued to thrive without detection.

In a white outfit, Wojciech had broken into the old de Luca family home in the town, shooting Papà in his bed while he'd slept. Teo had woken up from the sound of the gunshot, rushing in to see what had happened, finding Wojciech standing at the end of the bed, blood spattering his clothing, about to turn the gun on himself.

"No, that's not the way you're going to go out," Teo had said, anger so vile and penetrating he could barely see straight. Or that might have been the tears.

Wojciech had stared at him, and in broken Italian, said, "You will not tell me how I will die."

"Oh, I will."

Teo had run at him, smacking the gun away, tackling him to the floor. He'd strangled him, his favourite method, then drove the body into the forest and dumped him in a hastily dug grave. Wojciech had never been found, and the story was that someone had come to rob the de Lucas, Papà had woken and startled them, and he'd been shot.

A home invasion gone wrong.

The townspeople had grieved as if a king had died, the streets laden with flowers, mourners lining the pavements as Papà's coffin had glided past on its way to the cemetery. Whenever Teo went there to lay bouquets, several were already there, placed by unknown people who'd seen Papà as their saviour, the one everyone turned to when in need, Papà giving them money to help tide them over. All an elaborate ruse to disguise who he'd really been.

"If you behave as though you're an angel, figlio, they will believe it," he'd said.

Figlio, son, something Teo hadn't heard in a long time. He was thirty now, so it had been seven years. He'd taken on Papà's mantle, become even more caring than him, needing to secure the love and adoration of the town, to become their new angel, when behind closed doors he was a devil.

He'd sold the house and moved, glad to be away from the place where his mother had once lived, where her bitch feet had whispered over the floors, her bitch hands had touched the stair rails, and her breath, he swore, had seeped into the walls. Here, there were no memories of her, except the ones Papà had planted. Teo could see in all directions, and CCTV pointed everywhere, tracking any visitors. An office dedicated to monitoring, filled with screens, gave him peace of mind. No one was allowed here without an appointment, and it was well known that the only day he accepted visitors in need from the town was a Wednesday if he was in the country. While he was away, he paid Lorenzo to look after the place, an older local man, one who knew about

The Network and had worked for Papà, a loyal servant.

Teo thought about what was happening tonight in London. A new venture. Sex shows. The refugees would be having it away with each other on stage at a Mr Johnson's house, a long-standing 'User' of what amounted to prostitutes. Women forced into it. Teo didn't care about their feelings, just the money made from them. They were pieces of rubbish to him, easily discarded, easily killed. They were representations of his mother, reminding him of who she'd been and who not to trust. If they failed to bring in the highest payment, the best praise from Users, he ordered them gone. If they ever, *ever* got ideas above their station and tried to make the Users fall in love with them, they were dead.

More waited to take their places, although so many of them didn't know it yet. They currently lived unhappy lives, albeit free, oblivious to what the future held, wishing they could escape to numerous places around the world — where, unbeknownst to them, The Network operated. One day, if Teo's scouts, after watching the women, listening to them, approached and offered them the better life they so craved, they'd find out exactly what it felt like to land in hot water, what happened when they wished for more than they deserved.

Like Mamma.

Once they were convinced the scouts were genuine people who only wanted to help, they paid for passage to their chosen destination, thinking they would have jobs and be housed—promises, promises, lies, lies—and, once there, they discovered it wasn't how it had been painted to them by the scouts' silver tongues. The scouts and Network employees were Minions, as Papà had called them, something Teo had continued to do. By the time the women realised their dreams had turned into nightmares, it was too late.

Some would say a son finding out his father ran such an empire should be in shock, but Teo had been intrigued. Like Papà, he despised women who wanted more, who were greedy and unsatisfied with their lot, the same as Mamma had been.

She'd been buried in the forest, too, Wojciech likely bones now beside her.

A sour taste flooded Teo's mouth, as it always did when he thought of Mamma, the bitch, a refugee herself once upon a time, coming from the Eastern Block to Italy, one of Papà's recruited women so many years ago. She'd supposedly fallen in love with him, but it had been a ploy, a way to get herself out of the numbered rooms in the hidden refugee house here in Italy. She'd charmed Papà, pulled so much wool over his eyes he'd been blind to anything but her for a while, until he'd regained the clarity of twenty-twenty vision.

Teo had been two when Papà had killed her.

He stood, shaking off the anger, and decided to pack a bag. He'd go to the UK, to the first sex party to see how it panned out. If it was a success, he'd ensure every country in which he operated would also have them.

He checked the flights on his phone. If he hurried, he'd make the next one. He'd have time to get to his hotel, freshen up in the shower, and arrive at Mr Johnson's before the refugees turned up. He'd be cutting it fine, but he enjoyed the feeling that thrills gave him.

There was no other emotion like it.

Chapter Ten

Beaker had dropped Nan off at the train station. She'd been over the moon about the holiday, especially when she'd phoned her boss who'd agreed to her having paid time off. Those twins, everything went like clockwork where they were concerned. Beaker supposed it would, considering who they were.

I mean, look at me. I'm doing whatever the fuck they want. They just have to click their fingers and shit gets done.

Yeah, the money was a big incentive, but he valued his life more—Denny versus George and Greg... Beaker knew whose side he wanted to be on. Mind you, if that was so, why hadn't he told them about the other personality Denny had, the one where he was so much more than a man who was good with threatening words? The way Denny was at the house was different to elsewhere. He looked scary, as if something rotten lived inside him and festered, infecting him with a different attitude. It was weird, because it wasn't anything like the person Beaker had thought he was. You had to be well clever if you could hide your true self like that. Scheming. Controlled.

Could Beaker be clever now, hiding who he'd become? A little snitch?

Blimey, he'd never wanted to be one of those, but it wasn't like he had an option here, was it. You didn't ignore the twins. Not unless you were Denny and the like.

Beaker got out of the taxi down the road from the refugee house and waited for it to drive away, as he always did. Denny had told him to do that, although Beaker reckoned it was a stupid move because there was nothing else out this way but the house. The taxi drivers must wonder what he was up to being dropped off by a cluster of trees all the time. They could think he was some pervert who waited in the woods for dog walkers to come by so he could attack them.

He laughed off his stupid thoughts, a jittery laugh because he was on his way up the drive now, hands in pockets, trying to act casual. He wasn't sure he could pull it off, what the twins wanted, not when his nerves were strung so tight. He was bound to slip up, give someone the idea he had a big secret inside him. They'd ask questions, want to know why he acted so weird. Jesus.

He walked round the back of the house, same as always, and knocked the special knock on the wooden door that had no glass panels, just a spyhole. The blinds were down at all the lower windows, as usual, and no light shone from behind them as Denny had blackout curtains, too. Upstairs, wood had been screwed over the glass. To anyone driving by in the dark, the house didn't exist.

The door opened, and the other bloke who babysat with him, Chris, stepped back to let him in. He was a lanky kid, nineteen, a few scars on his cheeks from acne back in the day. Shaved hair, a number one, Beaker reckoned, a dip in his scalp at the top where he'd said he'd been dropped on his head as a baby, then he'd admitted it was a joke. Probably his way of deflecting attention, because the dip was a big one.

Makes me wonder why he shaves his hair, then. Likely thinks it makes him look hard to be a skinhead, yet he's soft as shit.

Beaker walked inside, took his jacket off, and hung it on the hook on the back of the kitchen door. His phone was in the pocket, and he'd switched it off in case The Brothers rang, something he couldn't be doing with while Denny was around, and he'd said so, too. He couldn't *not* play his phone, though, that would look suss, maybe set Chris off questioning him. Beaker would get it out later, once Denny and Patrick had gone.

"All right?" Chris asked.

God, had he spotted something off about Beaker already? "Yeah, you?"

Chris rubbed his jaw gingerly. "Not too bad, although I've got a raging toothache."

"You need to get yourself down to the dentist."

Chris locked the door. "Are you having a laugh? No one's taking NHS patients these days."

Beaker shrugged. "Dunno what to suggest, then."

"Paracetamol's keeping it at bay. Denny said he'd get me some Naproxen off some nurse he does dealings with."

"Ah right."

Beaker went to the meeting room where he had to show his face to Denny. Chris had followed him and plonked himself down next to Patrick. The boss sat at the head of the table, scowling at that woman who'd been living here. Beaker didn't know her name, she was called Little Thief, and he didn't recognise her either. She was a bit of a plain sort, no makeup, and she always disappeared upstairs to fix the girls' faces once he'd arrived. After that, she holed herself up in the smallest bedroom, and he never saw her come the morning.

She got up now, her head down, and closed the door behind her.

"Talkative sort, that one," Beaker said in his normal, light-hearted manner. He sat in her spot and folded his arms.

"She's been a naughty girl today. What have you been up to?"

The question shit Beaker up. "The usual, although I had a Chinese for dinner instead of chip shop."

"Been out anywhere?"

Beaker shrugged, bricking it. "Went to see Nan off at the train station before I came here. She's gone on holiday." The twins had said for him to stay as close to the truth as possible in case he was being watched.

Denny raised his eyebrows. "Anywhere nice?"

"Dunno, she didn't say."

"Bit weird, isn't it, not saying where she's going?"

"Maybe she did, and I wasn't really listening." Beaker shrugged again. "You know what the oldies are like, gas, gas, gas."

Denny laughed. "Hmm. The reason I'm asking about your day is… Have you spoken to anyone else other than your nan and those pricks on your Xbox?"

Beaker wanted to be sick. Fucking hell, did Denny know The Brothers had been to his flat? Was he testing him? "How come you need to know? My life's boring as fuck."

"Like I said, Little Thief was naughty today, and I wondered what the word is on the street."

Patrick clenched his hands into fists and seemed well dogged off.

"What's she done?" Beaker asked.

"Stolen a shedload of jewellery and happens to have got caught up in a murder at Vintage Finds."

Oh shit. Bloody hell. Little Thief was Macey Moorhouse? Jesus, he'd never have guessed. "Fuck me, she doesn't strike me as the sort."

"That's the beauty of it," Denny said. "We all wear masks, don't we. We all hide behind them."

What did that mean? Was Denny implying Beaker had a whopping great mask on tonight, one the twins had told him to wear? "Dunno, I'm just me all the time."

"Make sure it stays that way." Denny got up and patted Beaker on the head. "I quite like you, so don't disappoint me."

"Course I won't."

Patrick moved to the door like he couldn't wait to get out. What was up with him?

Denny joined him. "Right, I'm going home. I fancy a nice quiet evening in front of the telly."

This had worked out better than Beaker could have hoped. A location already, and Chris was here to take the fall for being a grass, although Beaker felt a bit bad about that.

Better him than me…

He itched to go and get his phone, tap out a message to the twins—George had put their number into his contacts—but he'd have to wait until he was sure Denny had gone. He got up and followed them down to the kitchen, reaching it just as Denny and Patrick disappeared through the back door. The lock engaging from the outside gave Beaker the sense he was caged in, never allowed to leave, and he shuddered, telling himself off for being such a pleb. Of course he could leave, a key hung from a hook on the wall. People used it when they went outside for a fag.

He took his phone out and wandered to the living room at the front. Listened for the car engine. It rumbled to life, then the crackle of tyres turning over gravel filtered in, putting Beaker's mind at rest. He nipped to the little loo and sat on the closed lid, shaking as he accessed The Brothers' number which was under the name Elsie, Nan's neighbour.

BEAKER: D IS GOING HOME.

ELSIE: CHEERS. GOOD LAD. DO YOU KNOW WHERE HE LIVES?

BEAKER: NO. HAVE TO GO INTO THE LIVING ROOM WITH C NOW, SO DON'T PHONE. WHATSAPP WILL BE OKAY, THOUGH. WILL PUT IT ON VIBRATE.

ELSIE: RIGHT. DELETE THESE MESSAGES.

He'd already been told what to do but was glad of the reminder. His thoughts were going haywire, not to mention his body felt weird, like it didn't belong to him. His arms had gone floppy, and everything was heavy, like he'd had dose of adrenaline dumped into him, sending him weak.

He shoved his phone in his pocket and rose to wash his face at the little sink, seeing as it had gone all clammy. He let the water run over his wrists, hoping it would cool him down and get rid of that bloody awful blush he always struggled with. That was the trouble with being a ginger, guilt always sent his cheeks red. Fuck's sake.

He dried his wrists and face on the hand towel and left the loo, wondering what time June would come to do the refugees' hair.

In the living room, Chris read a book, and he glanced up, frowning. "Fucking hell, what's up with you?"

Beaker panicked. "Eh?"

"Beetroot or what!"

"Oh, yeah. I feel a bit sick. Reckon that Chinese was dodgy. Probably the prawns. My stomach doesn't feel right."

"Go and puke then. Better out than in, that's what my mum says."

"Right. Yeah. I'll do that."

Beaker went back to the toilet. He pretended to be sick, did all the right noises, then sat for a while. He'd make out he had the shits if Chris asked why he'd been ages. He just needed a bit of time to calm down, that was all.

George and Greg were probably following Denny now, ready to ambush him once he'd gone inside his house. But what if Patrick went in with him? That could fuck things up.

But it wasn't Beaker's problem. He'd done his part. What more could he do?

Chapter Eleven

Oleksiy didn't like the woman who did the makeup. She was surly, snapping at them if they made conversation between themselves, saying they were rude to speak in their native language when English people were present— emphasising that as they lived in England, they should act like the English.

Oleksiy spoke the language well enough, she'd learnt it in her homeland, and she was teaching the others, the basics at least. So when Acid Tits, as Oleksiy called her, talked about them with the hairdresser, June, her words were fully understood. It was obvious the refugees weren't liked and Acid Tits was a staunch believer in wanting the country to have no foreigners in it. June was okay, though, she stuck up for them, had sympathy, although she was careful not to be too empathetic if Denny was around. Probably because if he found out, there'd be trouble. Oleksiy was surprised June let Acid Tits in on her true feelings. She must trust her to keep them to herself.

Oleksiy sat on her mattress, her back to the wall while June did Bohuslava's hair at the table beneath the boarded-up window, drawing it into an elegant updo that gave the impression Bohuslava had an extra-long neck. At least they were together, sisters in the same boat, although Oleksiy wished they were back in the *other* boat, the one they'd come to England on. The ferry. It had all seemed above board, nothing suspicious going on.

If she'd known then what she knew now, she'd never have got off, or if she had, she'd have grabbed Bohuslava's hand and dragged her away, running until they reached safety. They could have sought asylum. The legal refugee places here had to be better than this house. At least they wouldn't be forced to have sex.

Oleksiy had a plan. How could she not? She was prepared to wait until she and Bohuslava were taken to the same party so they could escape together. More often than not they were separated, but she could bide her time. They'd been here for so long and knew the rules, the way things worked. Silly, on Denny's part, to have not realised that caged animals always plotted how to bite through the bars, that some of them didn't become institutionalised. She watched, she sucked in information, and used it to her advantage. Maybe he thought the men who ferried them to the sex parties couldn't be persuaded to turn the other way on occasion. Maybe he didn't realise Oleksiy had been having sex with one of them and he'd assured her he'd set them free once he got the chance.

And maybe that man was lying. It was possible. She trusted no one here except for

117

Bohuslava, and any promises from Graham must be taken as empty, as hollow as her feelings for him, ones she feigned in order to get what she wanted. She loved him, she'd said. She wanted to have his babies, she'd said.

She'd lied.

"These fucking women should never have been so stupid as to get on the ferry," Acid Tits ranted. "Are they thick? Everyone knows you're either on your way to the sex trade or put in one of those manky places when you pay someone to take you out of your country."

"They were desperate," June said. "Only someone without a heart can have no sympathy. Can't you put yourself in their shoes?"

"Why would I want to? I've got shit on my own, let alone walking in theirs."

"Then maybe you should sort *your* life out before you cast aspersions about others. What's that saying? People in glass houses…"

"Fuck off. What do you know."

"I know that by me coming here, despite what they've got to do when they're picked up, they can at least go with a nice hairdo, they can feel good about themselves. Pretty."

"So that's the only reason you agreed to do it? Get lost. The money would have swayed it."

"I'm not going to lie, the money is good, and I know you won't believe me, but I really enjoy making them happy."

"What's Denny got on you? Why haven't you told anyone about this place and what goes on here?"

"He hasn't got murderer's assistant on me if that's what you're wondering."

"Whatever."

June glanced over at the women. "They change once they're all dressed up. Like they're not the dregs of society anymore but people who matter. That's got to be a good thing. It counterbalances what's going on."

Acid Tits scoffed. "You tell yourself that if it makes you feel better."

June was right. All of them appreciated the hair and makeup, even though it got ruined by pawing hands, wrenching hands. Once they were dressed and ready to go, although lambs to the slaughter, they *did* feel good, if only for the journey to whichever destination and, if they were lucky, during a brief moment they could look in a mirror at the fancy houses and see the masks Acid Tits had created, masks that hid who they were underneath. Vulnerable women, jaded, wondering if all was lost, whether there was any point in carrying on.

Oleksiy would never be defeated. She'd never have her soul crushed the way some of them had, girls who were no longer here, discarded, deemed the runts of the litter.

Denny had said they ended up in the woods, their graves deep, their presence eventually forgotten by everyone they'd been in contact with in England. But at home, they'd be mourned. Families would worry about the sudden radio silence, imagine their loved ones had perished at sea, begging the UK authorities to look for them, to find them, to allow them to go home. A mistake, they'd say, it had been a terrible mistake to let them get on that ferry in search of a better life for them all, where wages would be sent home to ease the burden. Please, turn back the clock, let us see them again.

Oleksiy blinked tears away. She couldn't afford to smudge her mascara. Acid Tits would get angry, and no one wanted that. Instead of morbid thoughts, scenarios she could do nothing about, she imagined her escape, Bohuslava by her side, the pair of them racing through the darkness, the scent of freedom in the air, in their hearts.

She had to focus on that. Anything else was too much.

Chapter Twelve

Patrick—or Minion-57 as he'd just said he wanted to be called now—made eye contact with Denny in the rearview mirror and cleared his throat. Denny wasn't about to call him that. He preferred first names and only followed the rules in front of Teo.

"I think we're being followed," Patrick said.

Denny turned, glanced through the back window, irritated that someone had the audacity to be right up their arse. A taxi, the light on top glowing. That wasn't anything to worry about, was it? Still, better to be safe than sorry. "Stay with me when we get to mine. Sit outside while I get changed. I'll go to tonight's party in case something iffy's going on. I'd rather be there than on my own at home."

"If we're being tailed, they'll see where you end up."

"If we're being tailed, you can take them out."

Patrick nodded. "Not a problem. I could do with some bloodshed. I've been wanting to try that gun out for ages."

"You brought it with you, then."

"Yep."

Patrick worried Denny sometimes. The bloke had been gung-ho when he'd first started working for him, too eager, but Denny had taught him how to behave, just like *he'd* been taught by someone in The Network. They had to smooth their jagged edges, be a bit more cultured. It was difficult, keeping tabs on your core being at all times, the very essence of you, even harder for Denny who had a few personas he had to keep track of. It was right, what he'd said about wearing masks. Before he'd gone into this line of work, before he'd done anything wrong, he'd have laughed if someone told him he'd be three kinds of people. Things changed, though, didn't they. Nothing ever stayed the same forever.

"How long have they been following us?" Denny asked.

"I didn't notice until we hit town and the taxi light went on."

"It shouldn't be a problem."

"Are you kidding? Haven't you watched that programme about the taxi driver who picked up women, drugged them, raped them, then dumped their bodies? Sorry, but taxis shit me up now, and I'd rather be careful."

Denny nodded to appease him. It was probably nothing, but he'd go to the party, even if only to calm Patrick's jitters. Yes, he'd wanted to go home and watch a bit of telly, be a normal person for once, but he lived in dangerous times, and that meant he had to do things he didn't want to every so often. He'd inserted himself into this gangster life, so he had to take the rough with the smooth.

"They've gone," Patrick said.

"Right."

"I feel better now."

Denny didn't remind him that the driver could have parked up down the end of the road, they could still be a threat. He didn't fancy the fallout of that conversation, and besides, no one should be following them anyway. Unless it was someone from The Network, nobody had reason to keep tabs on him.

"I've got to tell you something," Patrick said.

"Yeah? What's that?"

"I didn't want to say anything in front of the others, but I'm not best pleased about Angie. I thought she wouldn't get hurt."

"Ah. That. The plans changed at the last minute."

"So I gathered."

"I thought you couldn't stand her anyway."

"That's not the point. I've had Liv on my back, asking me to sit with her at the hospital. Her old dear collapsed. The shock about Angie. I'll nip to see her after I've dropped you off, then come back when you've finished at the party, but it might not be immediately. Because the *plans changed*, I've now got to explain where I'm going all the time, because, you know, it looks fucking off, me not being by my wife's side at the minute."

"Say you're letting the dog out."

"Already have—that's what I'm meant to be doing now."

"Then say you're needed at the pub."

"You don't get it, do you. Angie's murder has fucked things right up. I can't be at your beck and call like before."

"You'll work something out."

Denny had no sympathy for him. If Patrick wanted his wages, he'd do as he was told.

Patrick reversed into Denny's driveway, sighing. The house didn't look much from the outside, which was the point. He didn't want anyone knowing he was wealthy—yet—by splashing out on a new property. It was a red-brick effort, bought by his parents years ago in the sixties. They'd died, leaving it to him, and at the time he'd been grateful to not have rent or a mortgage to pay anymore. Instead, he'd used the money to tart the place up. Inside, it was tastefully decorated, mod cons coming out of his arse, an extension built on the back to give him more space, the illusion of living in the sort of house he *really* wanted. That would come, after he'd taken over Cardigan.

He got out of the car, leaving Patrick to keep watch. It didn't matter that the taxi had gone, he'd got himself geared up to go to the party now. Not to watch the sexual exploits, that wasn't his bag, but to mingle, to tell people who he was, that he was the man they needed to come to if they wanted private sessions with the women.

He entered the house, sorting the alarm, had a quick shower, and put on his best suit. As ready as he'd ever be, he returned to the car.

"You took your time," Patrick grumbled.

"Any sightings?" Denny slid his seat belt on.

"Nope."

"Good."

Patrick drove off, and Denny smiled. He'd get to see *all* of the girls in action tonight. This party needed the lot of them, many sex-obsessed people to service, lots of money to make, not only for himself but The Network. Weird how life turned out. Weird how you had to be in the right place at the right time on occasion to get to where you wanted to be, to get the prize you'd been hankering for, even if he hadn't known what that prize was. All he'd been after was more money, a bit of prestige, and to be approached by a scout in The Network had come as a welcome surprise. At first, he'd been a no-mark, someone who helped collect the girls when they'd been taken off the boat, the old boss of the East End area some ancient duffer back then. He'd died, though, and Denny had been given the chance to prove himself by taking his place.

So far, he'd done a bang-up job, so he'd been told.

The party house, large and imposing, seemed to glitter ahead in the darkness of the outskirts, all the many windows ablaze, the trees bordering the long driveway twinkling with fairy lights, an airport runway. Patrick drove round the back and parked—he'd get to go and appease Liv until Denny needed a lift.

Denny, pleased to note the minibus was here, the one that ferried the women, got out of the car and approached the open back door where a man stood smoking. He had the look of a butler about him, all tux and bow tie, although he wasn't one. He was a hired doorman for the homeowner, plain and simple, who smiled upon recognising Denny from the last party here.

"Evening," Jacob said.

129

Denny frowned. The twat had forgotten the 'sir'. He'd get that remedied. Denny liked being called sir, he felt important every time someone said it to him. He wasn't a lowlife anymore, scrabbling to make ends meet. He'd clawed his way up the ladder, and now look at him. It wouldn't be long before he could stop selling gear from the back of his car, his old façade no longer needed. People would sit up and take notice when he revealed who he really was these days. All right, some would laugh at first, wondering if he'd lost his marbles, had ideas above his station, but they'd soon see.

He entered the house, walking through the vast kitchen and into what the owner called the ballroom. It certainly resembled one. The high ceiling had a painting on it, cherubs and shit floating on clouds, and the wood-panelled walls, the sparkling chandeliers, if a bit poncy for Denny's tastes, gave the impression the room belonged in a palace.

It was packed, people milling about in search of someone to talk to, flirt with, others deep in conversation, champagne glasses held by delicate stems. Men and women, dressed up to the nines, making out this was any other normal gathering, when later, this lot would be naked and having sex in front of each other. It was a bit pervy in Denny's book, and he didn't engage in public sex, but this was the butter to his bread, and he couldn't let his personal feelings come into it.

A mini orchestra played on the round stage in the corner, something by Vivaldi—Denny had been listening to that sort of music a lot lately, forcing himself to like it. He preferred garage, if he were honest. He was a bit of a Craig David fan.

The big boss of The Network caught his eye. Teo de Luca, an Italian fella who resembled the bloke with the moustache off the Go Compare adverts, only slimmer and younger. Denny always expected him to break into song, but he never did—and thank God; that would be too fucking weird.

"Good evening, Denny." Teo's accent gave him a cultivated air.

Some people were just so *refined* without trying, weren't they? Jealous, Denny nodded. "Evening. Good turnout."

"More than usual."

"Hmm." Denny swiped a glass of champagne from a passing waiter. Sipped. This crap was nasty. He didn't understand how anyone liked it. Give him a nip of whiskey any day.

The Italian smiled. "Your girls look exceptional tonight."

Your girls. Denny puffed his chest out at that. "I've got a new makeup artist."

"And she's trustworthy?"

Denny bristled, wanted to say: *I wouldn't have fucking employed her if she wasn't, you dopey wop.* Instead, "Of course. Thoroughly vetted, like June."

"Excellent. We have a sex show arranged for them." Teo pointed to another stage at the back, rectangular, red curtains.

Sex show? This was new. The women usually copped off with whoever clicked their fingers, sometimes in public, other times upstairs in one of the many bedrooms where the true depravity took place. Customers knew if they went too far and a girl died, it could be hushed up.

"I look forward to watching it." Denny smiled to hide his distaste.

"A new batch is coming next week. Three are coming your way. I assume you have the room."

"If I don't, I'll make it." Denny disliked this part. Sorting the wheat from the chaff. Getting the weak ones killed, buried. It was all a bit of a faff. An inconvenience. There were only so many woods they could put the bodies in without being detected. They'd have to go farther afield at some point, which posed a greater risk of getting caught. Those bloody ANPR cameras were the bane of any criminal's life. Still, it was expected of him. He'd continue to do as he was told until he'd nabbed Cardigan. Once he ruled the East End, he'd jack this shit in. Maybe put Patrick's name forward to take his place.

"Exactly what I expected you to say." Teo shifted his eyes away from Denny, then held up a finger for whoever he'd spied to wait for him. "I must speak to someone. Excuse me."

He drifted off, Denny clearly not important anymore. That stung. Bugged the shit out of him. He plastered on a smile and walked to the edge of the ballroom, by the orchestra, leaning on the wall beside some tall potted plants. He poured the champagne into the mud, propped the glass between some leaves, and took his hip flask from his pocket. The whiskey took the edge off his anger. He shouldn't feel annoyed, Teo could organise whatever he wanted for the girls, but

Denny prickled at not being told about there being an actual show before now.

He'd have none of this shit when he'd claimed Cardigan. *He'd* be the one calling the shots. Until then, because he hadn't finalised his plans on the coup yet, he'd play the game.

The good employee.

Chapter Thirteen

*A*dults now, they'd been planning to leave for a while, the rumblings about all-out war seeming more than just rumours. It would be real soon, Oleksiy felt it in her bones, even though she'd tried to think otherwise. Her usual optimism had dwindled, a touch of Bohuslava's pessimism taking its place. It had crept up on her slowly as Chinese whispers had filtered in the past few months, her sunny demeanour cloaked with clouds, the surety that the storm would come filling her with dread. She now had a glimpse into what it was like to be Bohuslava, forever worrying, watching what she said, what others said, dissecting their words for hidden meanings, predicting the future so she wasn't disappointed when the bombs eventually rained down.

It wasn't just her. Many were nervous, hyperaware, glancing at people as if the enemy had been planted in towns and cities all over to spy, to gauge the mood, reporting back to their leader who waited for the moment to give the order to strike.

What Mother had said hadn't helped. "There are things we didn't tell you when you were young. About your father working in Kyiv. He wasn't there, he was in Moscow. He... He listened, he..."

"...was a spy?" Bohuslava had asked.

"Don't call him that," Mother had snapped. "He worked in intelligence."

Ah, that word sounded much less...illegal, didn't it? And that was that, how Mother knew the rumours were true because Father's old friend had kept in touch, warning her of an imminent attack.

"Do not tell anyone how you know," she'd said. "We could all be shot."

Oleksiy had lived in fear of the Russians because of her mother's tales, but Bohuslava was petrified of it coming to pass, someone entering their home at night and shooting them dead. Mother had insisted they leave, get out while they could. She didn't want them living under such tyranny, which was sure to happen if Ukraine was usurped.

"But what about you?" Bohuslava had asked.

"I will stay. I'll never leave your father."

"It's just his body. His spirit will be with us."

"No, I will not go."

Oleksiy blinked the memory away.

It was a cold February evening, two years after the start of the pandemic, and at five o'clock, she left the factory, tired after a long day. She walked through the centre of the industrial estate with the others who streamed along, heading for the bus stop, eager to get home. She'd meet her sister in a minute, who'd be around the corner near the other factory where she worked.

"It's only a matter of days now," someone said beside her.

Oleksiy froze inside. Did someone know Father's friend had warned them? Had he been sent to talk to her, to extract the friend's name from her so he could be caught for spying? She shot a peek at him, didn't recognise him from work, but that didn't mean anything. The factories in this town employed thousands, and he was just one of them. Dark hair clipped short, black-framed glasses, slight stubble, blue overalls.

If she looked for love, maybe he would be her type, but she didn't, so he wasn't. Not yet. Not until they'd got out of this country, settled in safety. The enemy had been situated at the border since last year, a hulking, loitering threat. Oleksiy and Bohuslava should have left then, when it was so clear what the future held. But they hadn't, they'd stayed, because it had felt as if they'd be abandoning Mother—and because Oleksiy had stupidly thought sending good vibes out to the universe would protect them.

Mother had quashed that line of thinking. "Remember, your father only said that universe rubbish so you wouldn't worry, but you're grown now, you need to face facts. There will be an attack, and no amount of pleading to fate will change that."

"We can't leave you," Bohuslava had said. "You have to come with us."

"No. No."

Oleksiy and Bohuslava hadn't saved enough money for the flights yet. This payday coming, they could buy

138

their tickets, hope for the best when they arrived at their destination, but would it be too late?

"Days?" she said to her new companion, her heart jolting at the idea they'd be stuck here. Father's friend had predicted a month before their world turned upside down.

Maybe flights would be grounded and no one would be able to get away by air. Maybe, if they travelled over land, and bombs rained down, they'd get blown up. What about the sea? Would the enemy be watching from the skies, from ships, from submarines? Would they be stopped? Killed for trying to escape?

"Yes," he said.

"How do you know?" She was naturally suspicious of anyone these days; he could be a mole, someone who spied for the spies.

"My father works for… He's in intelligence. That's all I can say."

"Intelligence." Like Father.

"I'm leaving. The day after tomorrow. Early morning. Going on a minibus to Calais then getting on a boat."

"Where will you go?"

"England. The people there will help us. I have a job waiting, a house."

Hope sparked again, and she felt like the old Oleksiy, the one who saw sunshine and rainbows instead of thunder and lightning.

"What job is it?" She wondered whether the English had big factories like here, whether she and Bohuslava could work there. Mother wanted them out of the country where she knew they'd be okay. They were leaving—for her. Not gladly. The thought of Mother being at the mercy of the Russian government who might find out what Father had done for a living…it didn't bear thinking about.

"There's a man called Teo, an Italian." He kicked at a pebble in their path. "He will be my new boss. I will be in a factory, like ours, a manager. A big step up from the line, eh?"

"Where is your new house?"

"London."

She imagined it, all those lights, all those people. The hustle and bustle, perhaps the same as Kyiv. Freedom from worry. But there would still be worry. About Mother, left here because she refused to go with them. She'd never leave her homeland, never. She belonged here, she said, where Father was buried, although she had promised if war did break out she go to Aunt Lyubov in the mountains. She'd be helped; already people made plans if they needed to escape. Car

140

shares, pooling money for fuel, all done on the quiet so anyone from the enemy wouldn't know Putin's plans had leaked somehow. When would the first strike happen? Where? Would it be one attack or many? How long would it go on for? Were the rumours even true? Was this fretting all for nothing?

How many would die?

"You could come, too," he said.

"I don't have enough money yet."

"How much do you have?"

She told him, for some reason embarrassed. Mother lived frugally off the life insurance. Oleksiy and Bohuslava didn't earn a lot.

"That's plenty." He smiled.

"Maybe for one person, but not two."

"Two?" He stuffed his hands in his pockets as they approached the corner.

"My sister. We must go together. Mother…"

"I understand. How old is she, your sister?"

"Two years younger than me." She pointed. "There she is, down there."

They'd turned the corner, and Bohuslava stood where she always did, blonde hair flying in the cold wind beneath a beanie hat. She was so pretty, delicate, the double of Mother. Her blue scarf flapped, and she stamped her feet to keep warm. A rush of love for her sister flooded through Oleksiy—if only they could leave now, tonight, get away from the fear, the anxiety of a brewing war.

"Ah, you look alike," he said. "I have enough money to help you if you want her to go with you. When you have a job, you can pay me back."

Oleksiy glanced at him sharply. "Why would you do that? You don't even know us."

"We help our fellow man, yes? Or women. We're all in this together."

"We have no jobs, nowhere to stay."

"I told you, I have a house waiting in London, you two can share a room. I'll be a manager and can give you jobs. It'll be okay. Do you want that or not? There are only three spaces left on the minibus."

"How come you know that?"

"Like I said, my father is in intelligence. He's organised my escape. He doesn't want me to go to war, to have to fight." He sighed. "They will be coming towards Kyiv, you mark my words. We won't be safe for much longer; we live too close to the capital."

They reached Bohuslava, who stared at the man, her eyes narrowed. She was more suspicious than Oleksiy, naturally anxious, always needing reassurance.

"Who is this?" she asked.

Oleksiy glanced around at everyone making for the bus stop at the end of the road. "He can help us."

"With what?" Bohuslava eyed him again, assessing. Worried.

"A boat. Going to London."

"We don't know him," Bohuslava muttered and walked off. "He could be one of them."

The enemy.

Oleksiy rushed after her, the man left in her wake. She tucked her arm around the crook of Bohuslava's elbow and whispered everything he'd said.

"Intelligence?" Bohuslava let out a scoffing sound. "And if that's true, we're supposed to believe he hasn't been taken away from here already? Intelligence sounds like his father is in the army or government; it sounds like he'd have sent his son away long before now."

"But you know how it's been. We've lived with the threat for years, same as everyone else. It's only recently we've heard the big rumours. And where have they come from, eh? They had to have started somewhere. Someone in the know must have spread them. We're believing those rumours now Father's friend confirmed them, we've been saving to go — why not believe the man back there, too?"

"We only have to wait until payday, then we can run."

"But what if that's too late?" Payday was on the thirtieth.

Bohuslava stopped and planted her hands on Oleksiy's shoulders. "But what if he isn't who he says he is? What if he's one of them? What if we're being tested, our loyalty? What if they know what Father did? And why did that man choose you to help? Why not someone else?"

Oleksiy smiled. "Maybe he fancies me, I don't know."

"It's not a time for jokes." Bohuslava stalked off again.

Oleksiy followed. "So you want to stay? Get bombed? Because they're coming. They're going to try to kill us all. What if, by the time we have the money, the flights are either booked up for months or they're not flying at all? What if we're stuck here?"

Bohuslava stopped again and spun, waiting for the man to catch up. She pointed at him. "We want to know the route, the plans. We're not giving you any money until we're on our way, and only half. You'll get the rest when we're on the boat."

He nodded. Smiled. "Let's get on the bus, go to a café. Talk."

Bohuslava glared. Assessed again. "There's no harm in talking, but that might be all we're doing."

Chapter Fourteen

George had parked in a lay-by, and they sat in the taxi, waiting. Denny's SUV had gone past, only the driver in it, a bearded bloke, so it was safe to assume Denny was in the big house. An Audi sped by, its indicator light flashing in the darkness. The car turned onto the long drive. George would like to wring that pervert's neck. Who the fuck went to sex parties? Who shagged women, knowing they'd been snatched off a boat, forced into this life?

"People make me sick," he said.

"Hmm. We're going to have to tell Janine about this. It's too big for us to handle."

While George would like to think they could handle *anything*, his brother was right. An organisation of this magnitude, the amount of people involved, it wasn't something they could stamp out, even with Moon's and Tick-Tock's help.

"Let's round Denny up first." George took his phone out and wrote a message to Beaker.

GG: ARE ALL THE GIRLS OUT OF THAT HOUSE?

BEAKER: YEAH. WE'RE TWIDDLING OUR THUMBS UNTIL THEY GET BACK.

GG: MESSAGE ME WHEN THEY ARRIVE.

BEAKER: OKAY. THERE'S SOMETHING YOU NEED TO KNOW.

GG: WHAT?

BEAKER: MACEY'S HERE.

GG: WHAT?

BEAKER: I DIDN'T RECOGNISE HER WITHOUT MAKEUP ON, BUT SHE WORKS FOR D. HE SAID ABOUT HER BEING AT VINTAGE TODAY. I SPOKE TO C, AND

HE SAID SOME BLOKE CALLED HONDA IS THE ONE WHO KILLED A.

George took a moment to process that, rage building. "Look at this." He showed Greg the message string.

"Christ. We'll have to get the word out, see if we can find this Honda fella." Greg clenched his fists. "We can't be in two places at once. It's Denny or Macey. Which one do you want to get first?"

"Denny. Maybe Moon will send someone to collect her for us."

"We're relying on him more and more over our own blokes."

"I know, but we all work well together, and I trust him, Alien, and Brickhouse to get the job done properly."

"But it looks like we don't trust our own fellas."

"We do, it's just…"

Greg grunted. "Christ. Want me to phone him?"

"Yeah."

Greg got out of the car and bent over to say, "I'll arrange for our men to be on the lookout for Honda."

George nodded, waited for the door to close, and got back to Beaker.

GG: SOMEONE'S GOING TO COME AND COLLECT HER. IT'LL PROBABLY BE MADE TO LOOK LIKE AN AMBUSH, SO ACT ACCORDINGLY.

BEAKER: FUCKING HELL.

GG: YOU'LL LIKELY HAVE TO TAKE A COUPLE OF HITS, SO IT SEEMS AUTHENTIC, AND VACATE ONCE YOU'VE SPOKEN TO D. THE POLICE WILL BE COMING TO COLLECT THE WOMEN.

BEAKER: RIGHT.

George slid the phone away. At least if Moon collared Macey and they grabbed Denny, the pair of them could be killed together. Two birds with one stone.

Greg got back in. "Sorted."

George got comfy. "Now we wait."

"We could have nipped off, you know, picked her up, then came back."

George shook his head. "I don't want to risk losing Denny."

"But we know where he lives now. He's got to go back at some point, get some kip. He's a sitting duck."

"Not if Macey manages to get a message to him when Moon storms in. He could go into hiding."

"Fair enough." Greg folded his arms. "We should have brought a flask with us. I fancy a cup of tea."

"Tough shit, you'll just have to have a mouth like a cream cracker without butter. Dry as arseholes."

Chapter Fifteen

Oleksiy wasn't prepared to go through with this, and she didn't have to. Graham had spoken quietly to her earlier, and although she didn't fully trust him, she believed him. Something in his eyes had told her he was being sincere. The man had fallen for her, that much was obvious, and she should be ashamed she'd used him, manipulated his feelings, but wouldn't anyone do the same in her situation? They were escaping, tonight, and he was going to help them do it.

She grabbed Bohuslava's hand behind the stage curtain and leaned close to whisper, "Come with me."

Bohuslava stared at her, clearly confused. "Why?"

"We're leaving."

"What?"

Oleksiy gave her a stern look. "Keep your voice down." She turned to Graham who stood in the wings and said to him, "We need toilet."

Graham spoke to the man with him, Vincent, who checked his watch and nodded. Graham beckoned to them, and Oleksiy tamped down the rampant butterflies in her stomach. She tugged Bohuslava to the side of the stage and followed Graham through a doorway that led into the large foyer. A burly man guarded the front door, and she glanced his way, but he wasn't interested in her, too busy spying through the ballroom doorway, probably anticipating the sex show starting. She swallowed her revulsion and went after Graham towards the big dining room at the back of the house.

Bohuslava squeezed her hand. "This is too risky. We'll get caught."

"But we have to at least try."

Through the dining room, and they came out in a hallway area the employees used. Off the quad-like space, closed doors with plaques on them. KITCHEN. OFFICE. TOILETS. EXIT. A key in the lock.

A key. Oh God…

"I'll wait here," Graham said.

Oleksiy nodded, recalling what he'd said earlier, what they had to do. He'd talked Vincent into ringing him so Graham would have to leave his post here. Whether that man could be trusted afterwards, she wasn't sure, but Vincent had agreed to keep quiet so long as he was paid well. And they had to leave now, while the sex show was on, everyone occupied by the women on the stage.

They entered the toilet, and she left the door ajar so she could hear what was going on. The sound of the key turning in the exit lock meant Graham had stuck to his word and opened it for them.

His phone rang, and her heart rate scattered.

"What?" he said. "Err, okay, but I've got two girls in the loo."

Was he saying that for the benefit of whoever might be behind the closed doors?

"I shouldn't leave them, but you're right, they're too scared to run." He laughed. "I'll be with you in a couple of minutes. Comes to something when you can't watch the punters on your own, mate. Yeah, yeah, I get it, the blokes look shifty and you want backup."

A knock at the door had Bohuslava whimpering.

"Do your business and go straight back to the stage," Graham said. "If you even think about legging it, we'll find you, and you'll be dumped in the woods, dead. Got it?"

"Yes," Oleksiy said. "Yes, we understand. We just want toilet."

"Hurry up," he said.

Was that for show, or was it an actual warning?

She pushed the door open and peered around it. No one was there.

"Quickly." She urged Bohuslava out and opened the exit door, staring outside, the patio lit with a security light. Graham had told her to run straight ahead, but what if that was a trap?

She decided to go the front way.

She stepped out, taking Bohuslava with her, and led the way past windows and the door they'd entered when they'd first arrived. The man who'd let them in wasn't there—Jacob, wasn't it?—and she went faster in case he came out for a cigarette and spotted them. Round the side, no lights, and she bent to remove her high-heeled sandals, bringing back a sharp memory of the pretty ones Father had bought for them so long ago.

"Get yours off," she whispered. "We can run faster without them."

"We'll be caught," Bohuslava said. "Graham will come back and find us gone. He'll raise the alarm."

"He won't." Oleksiy had to believe that. "He's the one who arranged this."

"What does he want in return? I told you to be careful with him. You're playing a dangerous game."

"Come on, there's no time to talk about it now."

They ran towards the front of the house, veering to the left on the huge expanse of grass, keeping to the darkness. She glanced back at the house which stood in bright light, and the trees with their twinkles, something she'd have thought pretty once upon a time but were now hideous. They'd always remind her of being here.

Fear spurred her on, and she clutched her shoes by the back straps—they'd need them once they hit a residential area. Adrenaline fuelled her, and she egged Bohuslava on, giving her sister courage, hope.

Trees surrounded the property, sectioning it off from the road, and Oleksiy ploughed between two of them, the soles of her feet sore from the rough bark coating the ground. They burst out the other side, and then the worry came. What if someone drove by, someone heading to the party? What if they were snatched and taken back to the house?

"Ah, лайно," she said. *Shit*.

"What?" Bohuslava asked, panicked.

"Nothing. Keep moving."

Oleksiy went left, and oh God, could it be true? Was that a taxi? She rushed towards it. She'd worry about paying the fare later. For now, they needed to be driven away from this hateful life.

"Get in the back," she said.

"But we don't know them. There are two men inside. What if…?"

Yes, what if…? Should they risk it? Had Graham ordered the cab? He must have and forgot to tell her.

"Trust me." Oleksiy wrenched the back door open, shoving Bohuslava inside, then she climbed in.

The driver turned to peer between the front seats. "Err, we're not working, love."

"Please. You have to take us away. Please, please…"

"Fuck me," he said. "Are you Denny's girls?"

Oh God. They knew him. She'd made the biggest mistake of her life, worse than getting off that ferry. "Please, he is bad man."

The driver glanced at the passenger beside him. "We're going to have to collect him another time."

"Yep. Get them the fuck out of here."

Bohuslava shivered beside her and grabbed Oleksiy's hands. "Ask where we're going."

"лайно." Oleksiy's mouth had run dry. She swallowed. "Where are you taking us?"

The passenger turned and looked at them. Oh. He was the same as the driver. Twins.

"Somewhere safe," he said. "Denny's got it coming, don't you worry."

Relief swam though her, even though a part of her cautioned that this could be a trick. Graham could have done this to show them, and the others, what happened when you tried to run. It could all be a cruel game to him.

"The other women," she said, "will you save them?"

"Us? Nah, but the police will."

She relaxed, slumping back on the seat. "Ring them now. Tell them. So we hear you do it. I want to speak to this police."

He faced the front and took the phone the driver held out. "Her name's Janine Sheldon, all right? Hang on."

He prodded the screen, held the phone up. It was on speaker. A lady's face filled the screen.

"Got a bit of a situation here," he said. "We've been given intel about Denny Rawlings."

"What about him?" the woman asked.

"Sex trafficking. Refugees."

"Bloody hell!"

He spoke to her for a while, and everything he said put Oleksiy at ease. They were safe, the police would look after them.

"I'll find Denny and arrest him," the officer said.

"No, you're to leave him alone," the passenger barked. "We'll deal with him."

"For fuck's *sake*, Greg!"

So that was his name.

"There are bodies," Oleksiy said. "In woods."

"What?" Janine sounded shocked.

Oleksiy continued. "They kill weak ones to make way for new. They are buried in woods."

"Which ones?" Janine asked.

"I do not know. Denny did not say."

"Do you know how many?"

"Twenty-three have been taken since we have been here. Me and my sister, we came for better life, away from the war. They said we have good jobs, we can send money home. The job is sex — we did not want to do that."

"Okay, listen, I can't go into details as to why, but when George and Greg bring you to me, if any other police officer queries it, you got into the taxi and asked to be taken to a police station, understand? You didn't talk to the driver. We didn't have this conversation. You'll act like it's the first time we've spoken when I meet you at the station."

Oleksiy panicked. "This does not sound right. Stop the car. We are getting out."

"Calm down," Janine said. "I promise you, this will all be okay. Greg, explain to her, will you? I've got to get myself down to the front desk so I just happen to be there when they come in."

Greg cut the call. "Look, she works for us. Long story. We'll give you all the details once Janine's spoken to you. We'll rent you a flat, give you jobs."

Oleksiy laughed. "We have heard that before." She sighed. "We do not believe in promises. Not anymore."

Greg turned and smiled at them. "You will. Have faith. We're your guardian angels."

Chapter Sixteen

Beaker, jumpy as hell, kept losing concentration on *Toon Blast*, a game on his phone. He'd been on the same level ever since he'd received the messages. He had a free hour of infinite lives, and he wondered if they'd be up before Moon arrived. Not knowing when he'd get here was doing a number on him. Waiting around for shit to kick off was nerve-racking.

Chris had his nose stuck in a book, as usual, and thank God he did. It meant he wasn't taking any notice of Beaker sweating like a bastard, his cheeks flaming from the guilt of knowing he was a grass. No one wanted to be called that, and although what he was doing was the right thing, his skin still had that oily residue that came with the thought of people finding out he was a turncoat.

He was dying for a Coke, but what if he went into the kitchen and Moon burst into the house? It would look like Beaker had opened the door to him, was in on it. He didn't like the idea of taking a few punches for the team, but if he didn't 'act accordingly', like he'd been told, Denny would ask questions.

He lost another level.

"Fuck's sake," he muttered.

"What's up with you?" Chris lowered his book.

"I keep losing."

"How's your guts?"

Rolling. Clenching. "A bit better, thanks, although I could do with going to bed. All that shitting's worn me out."

"I remember once, I thought my stomach had been turned inside out when—"

A loud bang. Sounded like the front door being busted in. Beaker's body reacted the same as it would had he not been expecting it—he let out a shout of alarm, and his heart thundered.

"What the fuck's *that*?" he whispered, tucking his phone in his jeans pocket.

Chris eyed the doorway. "Dunno. Maybe Denny's back, in a mood?"

"Should we go and check?"

Chris placed his book on the sofa beside him. "If he's thrown the front door open like that, he's pissed off, so no. I don't want to get in the firing line, you know what he's like."

"What if it isn't him, though?"

"Who else would it be?" Chris seemed to ponder that. "You're right. It could be anyone. Bloody hell…" He rose and walked towards the exit.

A big man filled the doorway. "Err, I don't think so, do you?"

He sounded American. Beaker stared at him, then at Chris who backed away, hands up.

"Who are you?" Chris asked.

"Never you mind," the mountain said. "Where's Macey Moorhouse?"

Chris frowned. "Who?"

"The bitch who does the makeup."

Chris flattened himself to the wall beside Beaker's armchair. "Upstairs. Did Denny send you to get her or summat?"

"None of your business who sent us."

"Us?" Chris craned his neck to look round the bloke.

Mountain came inside, followed by another large man, then Moon.

"Oh Jesus," Beaker whispered for Chris' benefit.

Cigar smoke wreathed the leader, and he puffed on his Havana, blowing more into the air. "Evenin'."

Chris gawped. "W-what...what's she done? The woman upstairs?"

"Not your concern," Moon said. "Now then, Alien's going to go and collect her, and you're going to stay here with me and Brickhouse. What's your name?" He pointed his cigar at Chris.

"C-Chris."

"And you?" He swung his gaze to Beaker.

"Beaker."

Moon nodded. "Right."

Alien walked out, and Moon closed the door. He stood with Brickhouse, smiling.

"Life's a funny old game, isn't it."

Macey had heard the bang but didn't take any notice. Shit always seemed to go on in this house, shouting, clattering. She'd had enough of being here, wanted to go home, and couldn't see why Denny wouldn't let her. All right, there was the obvious reason, The Brothers finding her, or she could run to the police, but that wasn't what she had in mind. Her plan to make out she'd been forced to attend the robbery had taken a firm hold, and she'd tell the twins her version of events and get them on her side.

The thud of footsteps on the stairs annoyed her. That skinhead kid didn't know how to walk quietly. He was probably coming up for a shit. That was all she needed, the smell of it wafting into her room.

Whoever was on the landing opened and shut doors. A momentary panic eclipsed her annoyance. Was it the police? Had they used one of those battering rams downstairs and that's what the noise was? Could she talk her way out of being here, pretend she'd been kidnapped and they were going to use her like the other women?

Her door flew open, and she jumped, sitting up in bed and staring at the bloke who glowered at her.

"Macey Moorhouse?" he said in an American accent.

Fuck. *Fuck.* He didn't have a uniform on but could be a detective.

"Answer me," he shouted.

She swallowed, nodded, clutching the thin quilt to her chin, feeling suddenly exposed and vulnerable.

"Get up," he ordered.

She pushed the quilt off, glad she had pyjamas on. "W-what's going on?"

"You've been a naughty girl."

She closed her eyes for a second. Opened them. "What?"

"Vintage Finds. The Brothers aren't best pleased with you."

Oh God, fuck. She must have been caught on camera, and the twins had recognised her, even with the mask on. "I was forced. Denny made me—"

"I don't give a fuck about Denny. You're my target for tonight. Get your things together, put your shoes on. You're coming with me."

She didn't have a choice here, and at least if she was being taken to The Brothers, she had a fighting chance. She stuffed her feet in her shoes, ignoring the clothes Denny had bought for her, seeing as she'd come here with nothing but what she'd stood up in. That she'd turn up to see the twins in pyjamas was the least of her worries. She grabbed her handbag and walked towards him. He stepped back, allowed her to come out, then gripped the back of her hair.

"Down we go."

"Ouch!"

He steered her to the top of the stairs and held her hair all the way down. In the hallway, they paused by the closed living room door.

"What about the other women?" she asked.

"Like you care what happens to them." He knocked on the door, then opened it, thrusting her inside.

She stared at two men—shit, one of them was Moon—then at Chris who had a black eye. He hugged himself on the sofa, rocking. She switched to Beaker whose nose streamed with blood, his top lip fat and split.

Moon eyed her, sucking on his cigar. "So you're Miss Moorhouse, are you?"

She didn't nod. Didn't bother speaking.

"You're in a whole heap of trouble, you stupid fucking cow. When will people ever learn, eh? The Brothers always catch up with you in the end." Moon turned to Chris and Beaker. "You should remember that. My advice is for the pair of you to get yourselves out of this mess. Fuck off, tonight, and don't look back. Unless you want the police on your arse."

Beaker didn't know if that was a proper warning or if Moon was just saying it for effect in front of Macey and Chris.

"What d'you mean, the police?" Chris asked.

Moon smiled. "Don't try to tell me you're thick up top. They'll be coming here, later, after the girls get back. Do you want to be arrested?"

Beaker wasn't sure what to do. He glanced at Chris.

"I'm staying," Chris said. "Denny will wonder where we are. He'll send someone for us, hunt us down if we don't stay."

Beaker, aware that wouldn't happen to him, kept that to himself, but he agreed with Chris. This had to look authentic, and while he appreciated Moon for the heads-up, even though one of the twins had already warned him, he intended to see this through as if it had been a genuine ambush. "I'll phone him, let him know someone's taken her, then we'll leave."

Moon sniffed. "Fair enough."

He walked out, his men following, Brickhouse dragging Macey behind him. Beaker remained seated, his nose throbbing, and took a picture of his face, then of Chris'.

"What are you doing?" Chris snapped.

"I'm sending the pictures to Denny so he can see we got duffed up. Fuck me, I can't stop shaking." He sent the images over WhatsApp, then waited.

The phone rang.

Beaker pressed the answer button and put it on speaker. "Denny?"

"Who else did you think it was? What the fuck's going on?"

171

"Some men came and took Little Thief."

"Shite. *Fuck*. That's all I need. Two of the bitches have run off, and I'm trying to find them. What did the men look like?"

"There were three. Big. I dunno, they were just massive."

"You didn't recognise them? They weren't The Brothers?"

"No, never seen them before."

"Why did they want Macey?"

"They didn't say."

"Fuck it."

"Look, we need to go to the hospital." He glanced at Chris to warn him to keep his mouth shut.

"I'll send someone round to take over. Leave the key in the electric box by the front door. I've got to go."

The call ended, and Beaker stuffed the phone in his pocket. He stood. "I don't know about you, but I'm off and never coming back."

"What? Denny's going to go spare."

"Didn't you hear Moon? What he said? *The Brothers always catch up with you in the end.* It was a warning, you pleb. They'll be after us if they find out we're involved in this. And do you want to get nicked by the police? I don't want to be here when they arrive, do you?"

Chris tentatively prodded his swelling eye. "But…"

"Sod this. You do you, and I'll do me."

Beaker walked out, going down the driveway, Moon's taillights at the end. His car roared off, and Beaker relaxed. He'd done what The Brothers had asked, and now it was their turn to uphold their side of the bargain. To pay him five grand, look after him, give him a job, because he had a funny feeling, despite the police being involved, that The Network might be paying him a visit in the not too distant future, and he'd need the twins' support.

Maybe he should move out of his flat. Dye his hair. Think of another nickname; he couldn't use Beaker anymore. There was no way all members of The Network would be rounded up tonight. Many lived abroad, supplying to Europe. It could take years for them all to be caught, and they could search for him.

In the meantime, Beaker would adopt another identity and pray the twins made sure he wasn't captured.

The crunch of gravel had him looking over his shoulder. Chris jogged towards him, slowing as he reached his side.

"I didn't put the key in the box," Chris said.

"Why not?"

"No point in the other two being caught in the house by the police, is there?"

"So you've got a heart after all." Beaker jammed his hands in his pockets. "Mind you, the door's busted. They could go in and get caught by the police anyway."

"Didn't think of that."

"Does Denny know where you live?"

"Nah."

Beaker sniffed then cuffed a fresh stream of blood away. "Lucky. You might want to think about leaving London, though."

"Why?"

"The Network…"

"Shit. Where will you go?"

"Dunno." Beaker wasn't about to tell him his plans. He *could* take Chris home with him, plead his case with The Brothers, but that would be pushing it. He had his own arse to save before he thought of anyone else's. At least the women would be rescued.

Unless Denny takes them to another location because of Moon nabbing Macey.

He had to remind himself that wasn't his problem. He'd done all he could, and now it was up to others to save the world.

They trudged down the road towards humanity, Chris huffing and puffing, likely trying to work out his next move.

"Got an aunt in Manchester," he said.

"Go there, then."

Chris scratched his head. "Probably best to. Do you really think they'll try to find us, The Network?"

"Do you want to take the risk? I'd like to think that as we're just babysitters, we're no one to write home about, but you just don't know, do you."

"What about Denny, though? Will he drop us in it when the police question him?"

Beaker hid his smile. "Nah, he'll be too busy covering his arse." *With the twins.* "He doesn't care about anyone but himself, and besides, if he tells them who we are, he'd be stupid. We could squeal, drop him right in the shit. He wouldn't want that."

"I hope you're right."

175

They continued in silence. Beaker was all talked out. He had too much on his mind and wanted to go home, crawl into bed, and hope no one came knocking. Maybe he wouldn't have to move. Denny didn't know where *he* lived either, unless he'd had Beaker followed. It could be like he'd said and The Network wouldn't bother with the likes of him. He'd heard one of the customers was a copper, so he'd be able to tell the others that no one called Beaker had blabbed. With Denny's mouth being silenced for good by George and Greg, there was nothing to worry about.

He had to believe that. He loved his flat and didn't want to leave.

They stopped at a row of shops in the East End.

"Look after yourself," Chris said.

"You, too. See ya."

Beaker went left, Chris went right.

End of association.

Chapter Seventeen

*T*hey'd travelled in the minibus for what seemed like forever. They headed for Calais and had passed through Lublin, Varsovie, Berlin, and were currently approaching Magdebourg where they'd stop for the night. They were to play at being tourists, they'd been told, twelve women in total. When asked by Bohuslava why there were only women, Isai, the man from the factory, had said it was easier for groups of the same sex to be dismissed, nothing to be concerned about. But why did they even need to be dismissed, she'd pressed.

"Because we're effectively fleeing our country. Do you want his spies to know we're on the run?"

It made sense to Oleksiy. After all, wouldn't it look suspicious if couples were running? Families?

"What about the men of these women?" Bohuslava had asked.

"They'll be coming in another bus next week."

"When we get out of Ukraine," she'd said, "we won't need to look over our shoulder, yes?"

Isai had nodded. "We should still stick to our story, that we're sightseeing. Spies are everywhere."

That also made sense, and in the end, Bohuslava had quieted, although Oleksiy could tell she was mulling it all over. They'd left Ukraine now, they were on safe territory in Germany, but like Bohuslava had whispered, "Think about what the Germans were like. We can't trust them. We can't trust anybody."

"But that was years ago, and you can't tar them all with that brush, just like we shouldn't lump all Russians together. It isn't right."

"Leave me to my worries." Bohuslava had held a hand up and closed her eyes.

Discussion over.

Oleksiy had successfully blocked out the tearful and heart-wrenching goodbye to Mother, who'd stood at the front door of their house and waved them off, mouthing, "Be free, go!", tears streaming down her face. Oleksiy couldn't think about it, not here, not when it could distress the other young women who'd also chosen to leave. If they saw her crying, it could set them off. Bohuslava didn't have the same courtesy in her. She cried whenever the fancy took her, said she couldn't help it, the emotions too great to hold back.

"What if it's the last time we see Mother? What if she goes to Kyiv, to Mezhyhirya, to remind herself of why we're doing this? Isai said they will head for Kyiv…"

Isai sat at the front of the bus beside the driver, Kuzma, who was a surly man and didn't speak much. He scared Oleksiy a little, all scowls and downturned mouth, and he grumbled a lot about being caught and going to prison. Oleksiy didn't understand why he kept saying that, or why Isai nudged him with his elbow and barked at him to shut up.

They could bicker all they liked. As long as Isai stuck to his side of the bargain and helped them all, that was what mattered.

They took a ferry from Calais to Dover, Isai taking care of everything. The Covid restrictions for masks had been lifted in the UK last month, but they all wore them anyway. Oleksiy agreed with Isai that it would hide their identities should they be searched for by the Russians. His comment had scared her, but could he be right? How far was the enemy prepared to go to make a point?

The women stuck together, like he'd suggested. If they wandered off and didn't make it to the minibus in time, he wasn't waiting for them, and they'd have to make their own way to London, then he might change his mind about giving them a job and finding them a place to stay.

They all hung on his every word, too frightened to disobey. Not frightened of him, he was a nice man, but frightened of finding themselves in a strange country with no safety net, hardly any money, and the confusion that always came with being somewhere new and foreign. None of them except Oleksiy spoke English. She'd been teaching herself more regularly ever since they'd decided to leave home, and while her enunciation was off at times, she knew enough to get by should they somehow become separated from Isai and the driver.

He paid for them to eat what was called a fry-up, and they drank coffee, then put the masks back on. Oleksiy totted it all up in her head, and with the rental of the minibus, the fuel from Ukraine to Calais, the overnight stops, the ferry fare…Isai must have used a lot of his own money to help them. He'd said she could pay him back, but she dreaded to think how much that would be. She'd researched London, it cost a fortune to live there, so she'd owe him for a long time on a factory wage. Still, she'd promised to take care of Bohuslava, and she would.

"Oh my God! Putin has attacked Ukraine," an Englishman said at a nearby table, his mouth hidden by a mask.

It was February twenty-fourth, 2022, and Oleksiy felt sick at how close they'd been to not getting away. But what about Mother? What did 'attacked' mean? Were soldiers marching, or were there bombs? She glanced at Bohuslava, who hadn't understood what the man had said, then she caught Isai's eye to see if he had.

It seemed he knew English by his scowl. He took his phone out and prodded at the screen. Oleksiy got up and stood behind him, reading the headline of a news article which was in her native language. Russian strikes and a large ground invasion had been launched. A northern front from Belarus towards Kyiv.

Bohuslava's words rushed at Oleksiy: "What if she goes to Kyiv, to Mezhyhirya, to remind herself of why we're doing this? Isai said they will head for Kyiv…"

"О, Боже," Oleksiy whispered—Oh God—and it drew attention to her.

"What is it?" one of the women said, eyes wide, hands gripped in a double fist beneath her chin.

Oleksiy didn't know what to say, so she sat, leaving it for Isai to explain, if he even would. He might think it was better to tell them once they were in the minibus so the people around them didn't stare their way. Everyone would cry, Oleksiy had no doubt about that, becoming hysterical at the thought of their loved ones back home coming to harm. Isai glared at her to keep her mouth shut, and for the first time, she sensed he might have a temper beneath his calm and kind countenance.

"Nothing," he said. "Just a bad weather front. Oleksiy was probably worried because we're on a ferry."

Oleksiy nodded to confirm his lie. Despite fear churning her stomach, and so she didn't have to make eye contact with Bohuslava who was sure to have picked up on the terror in Oleksiy's voice, she looked at the table. Bohuslava would pick apart what had just happened now, get herself swamped by an internal *frenzy, and she'd be a nervous wreck within five minutes.*

Oleksiy had to stop that from happening so glanced up at her and smiled. "You know I hate storms, and with the sea…"

"Hmm." Bohuslava eyed her, then stared through the window. "It just looks cold. No storm clouds." She returned her assessing gaze to Oleksiy. "When will the weather change?"

Isai butted in. "We'll be at Dover by then, so don't worry."

It took just over an hour and a half to get to Dover, and Oleksiy had never been so glad to be driven off that ferry. Bohuslava had gone into herself, and despite the terrible news, the worry gnawing at her, Oleksiy had come out of herself, safe now on British soil. Perhaps, now Russia had invaded, Mother would change her mind, would come to England, but was it too late? Would people be stopped from leaving by his army? Oleksiy imagined the scenario of Russian soldiers crawling out of the woodwork, their numbers so vast there were two soldiers to every Ukrainian citizen, on the lookout for people who had a mind to run. Would

Mother have already begun her journey to Aunt Lyubov's, as she'd promised if Russia attacked?

No one bothered with masks now.

Oleksiy closed her eyes, napping until Bohuslava nudged her awake.

"We are in somewhere called Canterbury," Bohuslava whispered. "And Isai says we need to get out and go in another bus. This one has engine trouble. Kuzma is swearing because he's running late to see his wife and doesn't want to stay around to wait for the new bus with Isai."

"Maybe his wife is already in England."

"But who will drive us if he goes to this wife?"

"Isai, maybe?" Oleksiy could drive, but she was unsure if she could handle a small bus.

She looked out of the window. They were in a car park, although it was empty, as if it wasn't used anymore. A building close by resembled a warehouse, the black eyes of its windows signalling it was no longer occupied—she had the sense they were alone here—and trees surrounded the area, slim white trunks with black gashes and bare branches. Birches. They reminded her of home, of 'the season of birch sap' from mid-March to early April, where gatherers looked for trees that would give the most sap, drilling a hole in each trunk and draining the sweet-tasting liquid to drink it, or they left it to brew, adding fruits which were preserved until the winter.

She swallowed a lump of emotion—she hadn't expected to feel homesick over a tree.

"What's wrong?" Bohuslava asked.

Oleksiy blinked her tears away. "I was thinking of the sap, how we won't go with Mother to collect it this year."

"We won't be doing many things, and it's better to go without the comforts of home than be dead."

Another minibus with tinted windows coasted towards them, and Kuzma remained in the driver's seat, Isai getting out and going around the back to open the doors. Oleksiy twisted to see him.

"We need to get in that bus." He gestured for them to get out. "Another hour and a half, and you'll be in London."

Everyone filed off and walked to the new bus. Bohuslava glanced at Oleksiy, giving her a look that said she was wary, but that was nothing new, she was always like that when she didn't know what was happening. Oleksiy remembered she hadn't given Isai the rest of the money on the ferry, so she fished in her bag and handed the envelope to him, then followed everyone in climbing into the fancier minibus.

185

All seated, she stared ahead at the driver and another man in the passenger seat.

"My boss will take it from here," Isai called from the back, and the doors slammed shut, the locks clunking into place.

Oleksiy manoeuvred round to catch a glimpse of him perhaps sitting in one of the rear seats, but through the window, she spotted him walking back to the other minibus, and her link to what she'd considered safety vanished. He'd been their organiser, their guide, and now he was leaving them? Some of the women shrieked, and others whispered amongst themselves, alarm clear.

"I said not to trust him," Bohuslava whispered. "I said, and you didn't listen."

"We all trusted him," someone said from behind.

The man in the passenger seat stood. Isai's boss. Teo, wasn't it?

He faced them and smiled. "Welcome to your new life, one that belongs to me."

Chapter Eighteen

Outside the party house, Denny was having a cow. According to Graham, Oleksiy and Bohuslava had gone to the toilet. Graham had been called away, swearing he'd warned them to go straight back to the stage, but the bitches weren't in the house, nor in the grounds as far as Denny could see. He peered around a wide tree trunk, thinking they'd be hiding there, but nothing.

The first he'd had heard about it was a panicked Graham flying up to him, saying they needed to talk in private, urgently. Denny had given him a bollocking for trusting the women to do as they were told, but he understood why he'd left them. Vincent had needed assistance with a couple of punters who'd appeared shifty. It was a good job he'd phoned Graham, because it had kicked off. The punters had tried to climb on the stage as soon as the curtains had opened. Vincent wouldn't have been able to manage them on his own. His instincts at spotting trouble before it started had been spot-on, as usual, but now the women were missing, and that posed a major problem.

Then there was the disturbing call with Beaker. Who the *fuck* were the three men, and what did they want with Macey? Or had Macey lied to him when she'd said she kept herself to herself, didn't have any friends? She might have phoned for them to collect her, acting out a charade, as if she'd gone with them against her will. If he found out that was the case, she'd be in the woods with the other slags, six feet under.

But what if she'd been recognised from the CCTV footage at Vintage? What if a police officer had offered up her name, having arrested her for shoplifting in the past? Her overbite was distinctive. Or had those bloody twins viewed it first, bided their time, then sent heavies to pick her up? How did anyone even know where she was?

Either way, there was a risk now, that Macey would tell someone about the refugee house. He wasn't worried about Beaker and Chris, they were sufficiently scared of him and would get patched up at the hospital, then go home and get some kip. They'd turn up for work tomorrow, no problem.

He calmed himself down, crashing through the trees in search of the women. Surely Macey wasn't stupid enough to grass him up. If she'd got mates to come and get her, she wouldn't say a word about Denny because he could open his mouth and blurt she'd been there when Honda had offed Angie.

It was useless, Oleksiy and Bohuslava weren't here. Now he'd have to return to the house and speak to Teo, tell him what had happened. Christ, as if he didn't have enough to worry about.

Should he tell him about Macey, too? No, Denny had sworn she was trustworthy. Teo would point out that she might not be, that Denny's intuition about her was way off, and then his position in The Network might be put in jeopardy. He needed the money he earnt from that to tide him over until he swiped The Cardigan Estate.

Fuck, he had so much going on inside his head it wasn't funny.

I should have stayed home tonight, then I wouldn't get the blame for this.

He headed for the house, thinking, plotting, working out how to spin it so he was viewed in a good light. At the back door, he glared at the butler-type fella, shaking his head.

"Aren't you meant to stand out here all night?" he barked. "What's the point of having security if you fuck off inside?"

Jacob spat on the ground. "I don't answer to you."

"Two women have gone AWOL."

"Not my problem, mate. My employer knows where I was, and he doesn't have an issue with his staff taking a piss."

"So you were in the loo, then?"

"Yeah."

Denny narrowed his eyes. "Which one?"

"The one downstairs was occupied. I went upstairs, not that I have to explain myself to you." Jacob pushed the door open.

Denny marched inside, angry at the ponce for having such a shitty attitude. When he ran Cardigan, if anyone ever spoke to him like that…

He huffed his way into the ballroom. The sex party was in full swing, people half naked, dicks and tits swinging about. It was gross, but he ignored it all and made for Teo who sat in a chair watching the proceedings, a hand in his pocket, probably tickling his cock.

Christ Almighty.

"We've got a problem." Denny wanted the floor to swallow him up.

Teo didn't look at him. "What is it?"

"Oleksiy and Bohuslava are missing."

Teo laughed and finally stared Denny's way. "So what? Like I said, new people are coming next week. I'll give you an extra two."

Although relieved, Denny worried why Teo didn't seem bothered. "But what if they talk?"

Teo smiled slyly. "Would you if you'd been told your family would be killed?"

Denny nodded. Stupid of him to have forgotten that The Network had tendrils everywhere and knew all about the women. Who they were before, where they'd lived. "You're right."

"Of course I am."

Dismissed by Teo turning his attention back to the perverts, Denny stalked off. Fuck this shit. He wasn't even supposed to be here. Graham and Vincent could handle the women, take them back to the house later.

Out the front, he messaged Patrick: I NEED PICKING UP.

PATRICK: I'LL COME NOW, BUT LIV WON'T BE HAPPY.

What the fuck do I care?

Denny slid the phone in his pocket and walked down the drive, keeping his eye out in case those two sisters were hiding, watching.

"You wait until I get my hands on you," he muttered.

Whores.

192

Jacob went outside and took the cash from his pocket. He counted it, smiling that he had indeed been paid two hundred quid by Graham to turn a blind eye. He reckoned the fella had a thing for the women and that's why he wanted to help them escape.

Money for old rope.

Chapter Nineteen

Teo remained in his seat, the sex show giving him the required anger to always hate conniving, greedy women, to be on his guard, to see behind the veils they constructed, ones they claimed were stitched with the promise of love, but in reality, each thread was spun from entrapment, a sticky web to ensnare. Look at them, pawing one another, although it pleased him they did as they were told, that they were too afraid not to. As Mamma should have been.

Papà had said she was the perfect refugee, learning how to behave, and quickly, she'd become one of the top-requested women, sought after, men fighting over her. Elegant, she'd taken to the life as if born to do so, had charmed them with her delicate accent and beautiful eyes, her expertise in the bedroom.

Soon, Papà had taken notice of how she was so wanted and had watched her in action, both in room THREE and with Users. Yes, he'd seen, then, how she could snag you with just one look, and he'd found himself thinking about her more than he should. He'd made the mistake of taking her for a meal, pretending he wanted to employ her as a madam, someone who the others should strive to be, learning Italian as well as she had, giving Users exactly what they wanted without complaint. She'd agreed she'd do it, she only wanted to please him, the great Edoardo de Luca, and she'd obey him without question until the day she died.

Those words, they'd wormed into Papà's head, and he hadn't wanted her to please *anyone* but him—no Users, *nobody*. So he'd taken her from

THREE and placed her in the family home, in a locked room which he visited night after night to see if his infatuation with her wore off, whether her sweet demeanour changed with her being on her own so much. After six months, his appetite for her had grown even more, she'd become sweeter, and he'd known he was in love with her.

She'd behaved until Teo had turned two, and then, thinking her feet were firmly under the table, she'd changed. Asked for things instead of waiting for them to be gifted. Poked her nose into refugee business. Made comments that no woman should—Papà had thought he'd taught her how it should be, but she'd slipped into her real self, showing that all along, her refugee façade had been a farce.

Teo hated that he was half of her.

He vowed never to let any refugee—indeed *any* woman at all—ensnare him like Mamma had with Papà. Whoever he settled down with eventually would be grateful for what she already had, she wouldn't want more, and if she asked for it, he'd set her straight, his hand clamped around her throat to prove a point. This was why he'd had the idea that he'd find a lover, a wife, in another country, one who thought he was a poor man, who didn't know the extent of his riches. Usually, once they saw euro signs in their heads, showing them what he was worth, it was game over. No, whoever he fell in love with would take him for who she thought he was inside, not what he could provide.

Although…he didn't think he had it in him to even fall in love. To trust. Papà's stories about Mamma had put Teo off, so he tended to sample some of the refugees when he got the urge to have sex.

He contemplated the missing women Denny had mentioned. He decided he'd scared them enough on the minibus when they'd first arrived in England so wasn't unduly worried about them talking to the police. Back then, he'd told Denny to bring the interpreter in to reiterate what he'd said to them, to ensure they knew their families would be killed if they didn't keep their slutty mouths shut, so why would they risk blurting the truth?

It wouldn't hurt to get hold of Minion-66, though, warn him to be on the lookout, and if 66 caught up with them, the message was clear: KILL THEM.

As for Denny's incompetence… This would be a test for the man. If he managed to locate the women and bring them back into the fold, Denny was a Minion worth keeping. If he didn't…well, there was always the woods.

Chapter Twenty

Oleksiy had finally calmed down. Janine was a real policewoman, and they'd given short statements and enough information for the police to look into The Network. Tomorrow, they'd be back to go over things in more depth, more names being given, but for now, they were being taken to a hotel in the back of Janine's unmarked car, and an officer in the passenger seat would stay outside their door. Janine had seemed alarmed enough about The Network to suspect they might send people out to look for them, and she didn't want to take any chances. She'd given them tracksuits from the police store, promising to buy more clothes tomorrow, and on the way, she stopped at a chemist, coming back out with brushes and toiletries.

Settled in the room, Janine leaving them to get some sleep, the policeman outside on a chair, Oleksiy had a shower while her sister sat in front of the desk and stared at herself in the small mirror. What was she seeing? The made-up face of a sex worker? Or something else? Her memories? Thoughts? They'd whispered in the dark at the refugee house, not wanting the others to hear about the lives they'd led before they'd got on the ferry. It was private, something they'd wanted to keep as their own, especially about Father being a spy.

Was Bohuslava thinking about their mother? Did she wonder, like Oleksiy, whether she was still alive? Was Mother fretting about why they hadn't made contact? Janine had sent someone to track down Mother's whereabouts. Why hadn't they got hold of her yet?

Oleksiy washed her hair, then her body, and it was so different from the showers at the house. Here, at least, she felt clean. She used the exfoliating side of the sponge Janine had bought to clean the makeup off, wincing at the pain but needing to scrub, to take off the top layer of skin. She dried herself with the white towel that was purer than she'd ever be, put on the complimentary dressing gown, and stared into the large mirror above the sink. She appeared haunted, and so she should. Hollowed eye sockets, the skin beneath a dirty grey from lack of sleep and proper nourishment. From worrying, night after night, whether the sex games would go too far and one of them would end up dead. That they'd be killed and buried in the woods.

"It's over now," she told the soulless woman staring back at her. "You saved your sister, like you promised."

She left the bathroom and brushed her hair, sitting on the end of the single bed. She'd insisted Bohuslava had the double.

"Are you okay?" she asked.

Bohuslava watched her in the mirror. "So Janine said, we are free. People will help us. Give is a house with a family until we can find our own. This country is helping the war effort."

Oleksiy nodded, tears burning.

Bohuslava let her own fall. "But we will never be free. Not in here." She tapped her head.

"It will get better. Go and shower. Someone will bring food, remember?"

Janine had also arranged that.

Bohuslava nodded and rose, entering the bathroom. Oleksiy stared after her, worrying if her sister was right and they weren't free after all.

Some scars would always remain.

Chapter Twenty-One

George and Greg had switched the taxi for a car their man, Dwayne, had stolen for them last week, then returned to the lay-by. The hope was that Denny was still at the party. One of their men sat outside his house in case he was en route there, and so far, no sign of him. Moon had taken Macey to his air-raid shelter, and the twins would pick her up in the morning. George liked the idea of her sweating it out overnight, bricking it.

To occupy himself, he thought about being Ruffian, the lone wolf who stalked the streets, killing to assuage his mad urges for bloodshed. He still hadn't confessed to Greg about it, had wanted to keep it to himself. Mind you, the need to share had been strong lately — they usually told each other everything. Greg would understand why George went out to kill, but he *wouldn't* understand why he wanted to do it alone. He'd probably be hurt George had seemingly cast him aside, that he even *wanted* to do something without his twin. It was going to be hard to explain to him that he'd been proving a point to himself, and Janet, the woman he'd been dating. Although she wasn't aware of his little killing side game.

She thought George had something *wrong* with him and wanted to label him with a diagnosis. She'd suggested George's mad side controlled him, not the other way round, and with Ruffian, he was showing himself *he* was in control. *He* chose what he did or didn't do.

He didn't think anyone would understand unless they were like him, so maybe there wasn't any point in explaining. He became Ruffian on the evenings he took Janet out for meals, dropping her home, doing some prowling and killing in disguise afterwards, then going home as if nothing had happened.

The past two weeks, Janet had become an irritating issue. She was more therapist than girlfriend lately, and sadly, he'd come to the conclusion that she wasn't for him after all. He'd imagined loving her, and wondered if he did, even just a bit, but her constant pecking about him accepting he had a problem with his mental health had worn thin. Shame. He'd had high hopes.

"I'm going to ditch Janet," he blurted.

Greg snapped his head round to stare at him. "You what?"

"You heard. She's getting on my nellies."

Greg laughed, a proper belly one. "I wondered when you'd see the light. Took you long enough."

George folded his arms, in a grump now. "What do you mean?"

"I've always felt there's something off about that woman. You're a subject to her, a project to fix. Why d'you think I got arsey when you kept going out with her? All right, I didn't like being left on my own, but the main thing was I could see how she was trying to mould you. *I've* accepted Mad George because I love you as you are, so why can't she? Why attempt to change you? Jesus, I've tried, and it doesn't work."

Well, George hadn't expected this. He felt a right plonker, not seeing the full picture all along. He had now, so that was something, but he'd never seen himself as the type to have the wool pulled over his eyes by a woman. He thought about the things he'd said, the shit he'd tossed around in his mind. He'd been prepared to kill whoever hurt Janet and reckoned that meant his feelings were getting stronger in the romance direction, but now he thought about it, he'd kill for *anyone* he cared about—and that's all it was with Janet, caring.

She'd been good to him, as his therapist at first and then his lover, but he should never have allowed himself to get involved with her outside the counsellor/patient setting. When it had become clear she was far too eager to get him to see her side of things, he'd had the urge to run. To back off. Whoa, woman, calm your tits. Yet he'd still continued taking her out for meals, although he *hadn't* taken advantage of the sex on offer recently. That would be cruel.

"Why didn't you say something?" he asked. "Why didn't you tell me I was being a complete knob?"

Greg pinched the bridge of his nose. "Because, as usual, you wouldn't have listened. You always have to find things out for yourself, can't take my word for it. And you were caught up in her, and I had to let it run its course. I cringed every time she told you off—you'd have said she was looking out for you, but no, she was controlling. She's not your mother and shouldn't act like one. She speaks to you like you're five, and while we're on the subject, she's pushy. Keeps on and on, expecting you to give in."

"I've noticed. Thing is, I think she loves me."

"It'll sting when you tell her it's over, then."

"Hmm."

Now George had to think of how he could go out as Ruffian. He wouldn't have Janet as an excuse anymore. Should he reveal his secret?

He took a deep breath. "I've been lying to you."

"I know."

"What?" George scowled at Greg.

209

"I always know. Come on, out with it. I *knew* there was something iffy with you but I put it down to Janet."

George shouldn't be surprised. He thought he'd been clever, hiding shit. When would he learn that his twin could read him like a book? "You'll be angry."

"I might not. Depends what it is."

Bloody hell, how could he put it? He thought about when he'd killed that bloke in an alley, strangling the fucking life out of him, then, when someone else had come along, he'd killed *her*, too. A woman with *kids*, for Pete's sake. He'd told himself that she was a dirty druggy, she didn't deserve children, and they'd be better off without her. He had to be careful. Ruffian entertained the red mist a bit too much. "You know those murders, those drug buyers…"

"Which ones? London's full of the fuckers." Greg frowned, thinking, and his eyebrows shot up, as if George's brain had connected to his and whispered who he meant. "Oh, fuck me, not Dean Matson and Laura Wilson?"

"Yeah."

"Christ, does Janine know?"

"Does she fuck."

"Why did you kill them?"

George shrugged. "Just wanted to."

"Oh, it's like that, is it."

"Yeah."

"Then I get it. What Mad George wants... What I *don't* get is why you did it by yourself."

"I *knew* you'd be mardy about that."

"I could have helped you. Made sure you kept yourself safe."

"You sound like Janet, saying you're only thinking of my best interests. I don't need help."

"Fair enough."

They stared ahead. George counted to thirty, waiting for his brother to pipe up again, which he would. The cogs would be turning, and he'd—

"How many more have you done since?" Greg asked.

There you go, he's off. "A few."

"A few? How many more do you have planned?"

"I don't plan it, I prowl, pick someone. Not just anyone, they've got to be scum or up to shit."

"And what, you just leave the bodies where you killed them?"

"Sometimes I hide them. On other estates."

211

"Oh my sodding *God*. On other *estates*? Are you mental? Don't answer that..." Greg let it percolate some more. "I hope you haven't dumped them on Moon's or Tick-Tock's because that's a cunt's move."

"Of *course* I bleedin' well haven't, they're our mates."

"At least you've retained some morals. I don't need to tell you how risky this is, especially with Janine not in the know. How can she cover for you? Jesus, bruv."

"I know."

"Be careful."

"Will do."

So that was it? Greg was giving him the green light to be Ruffian? He wasn't too pissy about it? To be honest, he'd sounded tired, as if George's antics were wearing him down. Or maybe he hadn't given him a bollocking because that was what Janet would have done and he sensed George didn't need that shit.

"When are you telling her? Janet?" Greg leant an elbow on the door and propped his head up. "And what the hell excuse are you going to give?"

"The truth. That she's getting on my pip, trying to boss me about, and I warned her not to, but she didn't listen."

"D'you reckon she'll take it well?"

George recalled two nights ago, when he'd whisked her to one of those crappy shows she loved, a musical, all that singing and dancing bollocks. He'd gone to them with her to prove he was prepared to bend, to share her passion, but ruddy Nora, he'd been bored off his knackers and wished he was at home with Greg. He knew for certain, then, that she wasn't the one for him. No matter what they were doing, where they went, it shouldn't matter so long as he was with her, but it *did* matter, and he'd found himself questioning their relationship.

"What's up?" she'd whispered as someone had wailed the line to a song on stage.

"To be honest, love, I'm bored."

"Oh, well, if I'm keeping you, feel free to fuck off."

He'd always admired her balls, the way she didn't care who he was, and the fact she wasn't afraid of him, but that night it had rubbed him up the wrong way—it had nudged Mad George, and Ruffian, into a bad mood, and he'd known she

213

wasn't safe around him anymore. She didn't get it, did she. There he'd been, sitting through something he detested — again, for her — yet when had she done something *he* liked? When had they shot pool or watched a film he'd picked? When had *she* bent to please *him*?

That wasn't fair. She had bent. She'd accepted what he did, why he did it, and she'd worked around that. God, what a mess. The problem was, now she'd narked him a few times, whenever he thought about her, he got pissed off. Everything about her grated, and it wasn't fair to keep going when he felt that way.

He remembered Greg had asked him a question. "She'll probably make out she's not bothered. Tough exterior an' all that."

"I thought you'd get married, you know."

"So did I, eventually, but it was more along the lines that I got swept up in the progression of things, that the next step was to meet her down the end of the aisle. I forgot myself, that I didn't *have* to conform. But it's like you said, having women in our lives, it's a pest, isn't it."

They laughed. Until they didn't.

The SUV coasted by and stopped at the end of the driveway two hundred metres ahead. Denny appeared from out of the trees, the headlights shining on him, and although they were far back enough not to be spotted, George still worried because Denny stared their way. He got in the car, and it drove off.

"He's going to clock us if we follow too closely," George said.

Greg slapped his thighs. "I've already sorted someone to wait at the refugee house."

"When did you do that? You didn't tell me!"

Greg smiled. "And you didn't tell me about your murder spree, so shut your fucking face."

George started the engine. "Dickhead."

"Ball bag."

George eased out of the lay-by, taking it slow. Whoever waited at the refugee house would let them know if Denny went there, and if he chose to go home, they'd also be informed.

"He might go to a boozer," George said.

"If he does, then we nab him later. He's ours whichever way you want to look at it."

George nodded in answer. He felt lighter now he'd got his worries off his chest. He'd speak to Janet once this was all over, reminding her that if she ever thought about going down the revenge route to get back at him, he'd have her sorted. She wasn't the type to grass him and Greg up to the police, but it didn't hurt to warn her, did it. This would be a lesson to her: *Don't try to change what doesn't want to be changed.*

He drove on, the SUV's taillights now specks in the darkness. Let Denny think he wasn't being followed. He'd soon see he was wrong.

Chapter Twenty-Two

*T*heir passports had been confiscated, as had their phones and bags, although the boss hadn't said why; he'd ignored all their questions, perhaps because he couldn't understand their language. Oleksiy had memorised his words from the minibus and, once they'd been left alone, she'd gone over what he'd said after they'd been taken to a house seemingly in the middle of nowhere and placed in a room with ONE on

217

a plaque on the door. Twelve of them, crammed onto mattresses with thin quilts and a few pillows, people having to share, to top and tail later when they slept.

If they even slept.

How had it come to this? Why had Isai fooled them so wickedly? For money? Or was this where they were supposed to live; was this the place he'd said he'd find for them? Oleksiy had imagined a bedroom in a small flat she and Bohuslava would share, not one with all the others. It was obvious, from what Teo had said, that they would work for a roof over their heads and food, nothing else. No wages in their hands to send home to their loved ones. Nothing for nice clothes—they would be provided and could only be worn when going to work. Fancy dresses, high heels, and people would come to do their hair and makeup. Why would they need all that while working in a factory? It didn't make sense.

It had to have been at least two hours since they'd arrived. The door was locked, many of them had tried to get out, and the window was boarded with wood. The radiator didn't let off much heat.

Later, men would arrive to show them what their work entailed, and she supposed they'd be taken to the factory for training.

She had yet to tell everyone about the Russian invasion and supposed, to take their minds off being stuffed in this room, she'd best do it now. Better to get it over and done with so when it came time for the men to come, they'd have cried it out of their systems.

"There's something else," she said, feeling guilty for keeping it a secret. "His army has attacked in Belarus, and they're heading to Kyiv."

"What?" Bohuslava screeched. "So this is the storm, eh? This is the lie on the ferry?"

Oleksiy nodded. "I didn't want us to draw attention."

Questions tumbled at her, but she didn't have any answers.

"I don't know," she said, hand raised. "That's all I saw on Isai's phone, nothing more."

Wails and tears, women drawing their knees up and clutching them, heads bent, awful noises coming out.

Someone said, "We would have been better to stay than be here with that man. That boss. If this was safe, we wouldn't be locked in. You hear about what goes on. Sex trafficking. Stupid people like us paying money for jobs, and when they get there, it's this...this!"

Oleksiy leant against the wall and closed her eyes, tried to shut out their ramblings, their crying, but most of all, she tried to drown out the voice of her sister

219

which floated in her head from nowhere, an accusation that Oleksiy had talked her into this, and now look where they were.

"I'll fix this," Oleksiy whispered. "I'll fix this, I swear."

A man called Denny told them some terrible things, like how he knew where their families lived, how easy it would be for Isai, when he arrived back home, to find them, kill them. Children, he'd said, would be slaughtered, their heads put on spikes, pictures of them sent to him so he could show any disbelievers that they needed to believe, that every word he spoke was true. He struck fear into them with every last word, every swipe of his hand through the air to emphasise the points he made.

In short, they were prisoners, and if they didn't do what he said, their families would die. Their work would sometimes involve being left alone with members of the public, but if they thought of asking for help, Denny would be told. He'd know.

"So..." He paced in front of the door in the only open space in the room. "That's the score."

A male interpreter translated for him, and even though Denny had told them to remain quiet while he laid down the law, some women still shrieked in horror. He'd yet to tell them what their jobs were, and despite what someone had said about sex trafficking, Oleksiy chose her father's route and opted for looking on the bright side. She'd find a way to escape this, she would, no matter that Bohuslava mumbled about how useless it all was, how they were stuck here forever.

A bearded man with a gun watched them, his cock hard behind his blue jeans. Oleksiy looked away, disgusted he could be turned on by words of violence, threats so evil no man should be aroused by them.

"A couple of men will be up here shortly. I'll leave Patrick here to look after you and make sure you behave when you're being taught what's what."

Oleksiy didn't want a job, not like that. Her cheek throbbed from being slapped, and a bruise formed on her ribs, black, so inky it resembled hot tar. The man who'd chosen her had punched her there, his fist so wide and big, the pain so crippling she wondered if he'd cracked something. The men had forced themselves on the women while the other captives watched, dreading

221

their turn. Screams, so many screams, and howls like Oleksiy had never heard before, people's souls being destroyed, their hopes dashed, their reason for living being tested.

As a woman, Oleksiy had always feared being raped, had imagined it, the terror, but the reality was so much worse than anything she could have conjured up in her mind. The violation had changed her from the moment her man had climbed on top of her, his face looming above, his teeth bared in a smile, his hot breath fanning her face. All the while, Bohuslava had been on the same mattress, clutching Oleksiy's hand for support, whispering nursery rhymes from their childhood, ones Father used to sing to them as he'd swung them around in the air.

Those songs had enabled Oleksiy to take herself away—probably the reason Bohuslava had sung them, to not only spirit herself from this room but Oleksiy, too—and she'd found herself in the garden at home, back to that day Father had arrived as a surprise, the food, the laughter, her parents merry drunk. It had been a beautiful day, the best, and it had got her through the brutal assault.

Enduring Bohuslava's rape had been worse than suffering her own. The mattress jostling, Bohuslava's nails digging into Oleksiy's hand, her sister's eyes scrunched shut, then opening at the point of penetration to stare directly at Oleksiy and tell her silently that this was Hell, they'd died, perhaps on the ferry in the storm she'd lied about, and ended up here, being violated, shown what they'd have to do night after night from now on.

No one had been punched in the face. Slaps, yes, but they only produced red marks which would fade. They had to remain pretty, although, the man with the gun had said as he'd shown the men out, makeup could work wonders.

Food had come. McDonald's, a little cold where they must have had to travel to collect it. She suspected having it delivered might bring on raised eyebrows from whoever dropped it off. That many bags wasn't normal. They ate their fill, another bout of nostalgia hitting Oleksiy because the food tasted exactly the same as at home. Of course it did, but still, a pang of wishing they'd never left hit her. Then a thought came, one she maybe shouldn't have entertained, one she'd never voice to the others.

Wasn't this better than being blown up by a bomb?

She wasn't sure. Didn't know if she'd prefer to be dead than touched, used like that again—and for however many other nights in the future.

"I will never trust anyone again," Bohuslava whispered beside her now, in the dark, the others sleeping.

"Not even me?" Oleksiy's bottom lip trembled.

"I don't know anymore. I don't know."

Chapter Twenty-Three

Macey couldn't believe she'd been placed on a table, her wrists and ankles held at each corner by manacles. Moon had said he'd be nice to her and not raise the tabletop. Apparently, it was a torture device, and if she pissed him off, the tabletop could be tipped forward so it was as if she stood, and she'd hang there for hours. He'd seemed to take great pleasure in informing her that the manacles would cut into her wrists eventually. She didn't want to piss him off, far from it. She wanted him on her side so he could talk to The Brothers on her behalf. He'd said they were good friends. When were they coming? Moon had mentioned they'd be here, although he'd given no indication when.

He sat on a sofa at the end of the weird room, an air-raid shelter, so she'd gathered as he'd opened the hatch and instructed her to go down the stairs. She'd have to lift her head and look past her feet to see him, but holding it up for too long had hurt her neck earlier. Instead, she closed her eyes. The spotlight trained on her was too harsh, too painful.

"I'm a good employer," he said. "I'm that nice, I'm sitting here while my men have a little kip. They've been on the go all day, see, doing a job for me, and we thought we were finished, but when The Brothers call, we never refuse. I could be sitting with my girlfriend, Debbie, cuddled up on the sofa, a film on, a bowl of popcorn between us, but no, you had to go and rob the twins' shop, so here I am, doing them a solid. I should punch you just for fucking up my evening."

The worst had happened, but she should have known. All those cameras… "How did they know it was me?"

He chuckled. "You were a prick and didn't cover your beauty spot, and as for those gnashers of yours… Ever thought about getting a brace? Obviously not. George recognised you from the footage when you nicked that necklace last week."

Oh God. She'd had makeup on then and had enhanced the beauty spot with kohl. And as for today, that was Denny's fault. He'd told her to wear no makeup because she'd have that Zorro mask on, so she hadn't been able to put concealer on to hide it.

"I didn't kill Angie, though, that was nothing to do with me," she said.

"I know, but you were there, an accomplice, so in the police's eyes, you'd still get done for murder by association—they call it joint enterprise. Lucky for you, the police won't know you, specifically, had anything to do with it, they just know a woman was present—they've got the CCTV, but their copper will steer the investigation to a dead end. George and Greg know you only stole the jewellery. Still, that's a black mark against you. That gear was worth a fair bit, so I'm told. What possessed you to go through with it?"

"Nothing possessed me. Denny forced me into it. I've been stuck at that house for days. He said if I used my phone and asked for help, he'd kill me."

"And you believed him?"

"He can be scary when he wants to be, and after Honda slit Angie's throat, yeah, I believed him."

"Honda, eh? That's a name you won't forget. Where does he live?"

"Fuck knows."

"I'll let the twins know about him, just in case they don't know."

It went quiet. He must be messaging them.

She was relieved Moon was prepared to listen to her. He was right, stealing that jewellery *was* a black mark, but what could she have done? Honda had a shotgun, and he was that loopy, he'd have probably used it on her if she'd tried to run. Just imagine if she'd legged it when they'd left the shop, darting into the crowd of shoppers, and he'd fired. He could have hit an innocent person. Okay, she wouldn't have cared, she'd have just been glad to get away, but now, in the face of being held captive, she felt a bit bad about certain things.

Yet she couldn't deny smiling when she'd spied those jewels. For a moment, it was as if she'd been alone, seeing the spoils, calculating how much they were worth, who she could have sold them to, all that money she'd have made. Then she'd remembered Honda stood there, and she'd sobered. After that, it had all gone so fast. She wasn't even sure about the order of events anymore. She was tired, her mind sluggish.

"They're already aware of him," Moon said. "No harm in making sure, though, is there."

"Who told them?"

"That Beaker kid. He works for them. Did you know that?"

"*What*?" She snapped her eyes open, blinked from the horrible brightness, and closed them again. She laughed, the sound gurgling in her throat. "Bloody hell, I'd like to be a fly on the wall when Denny finds out."

"I expect you will be. I've got to take you to the warehouse in the morning."

Her heartbeat flickered. "The warehouse?"

"Hmm."

"W-where's that?"

"The East End. Belongs to The Brothers."

Oh God, what were they going to do to her? "Is...is Denny there?"

"He will be by then. They're in the process of collecting him, hence George telling me to fuck off because they're busy. He's a hard bastard, one of the meanest fuckers you'll ever meet if you get on the wrong side of him. On the other hand, he can be sweet and caring if you're in his good books. Shame you're not." The sound of a drink being poured. The click of a lighter.

He's lit that bloody cigar again.

"They've been looking for you all week." Moon's tone had changed. He didn't come across as pleasant anymore.

Should she be worried? Would he dare hurt her when she was the twins' captive? Yes, she was on Moon's property, but they'd see it as her belonging to them. Or had Moon been given permission to do whatever it took to get information out of her? She thought about being hit with the mallet he'd mentioned earlier and grimaced.

"Denny said they had," she managed, voice wobbly.

"Ah, so he's had his ear to the ground. Sensible. He's not a complete cockwomble, then." A pause. "They know you nicked that necklace, that you went to Bumble's Café and phoned Denny, tried to get him to buy it."

This was getting worse. "How?"

"One of their women followed you. Angie recognised you when you legged it out of the shop, and Zoe, who was out the back, went after you. She's a good girl, Zoe."

It must have been that bitch who'd earwigged her phone conversation. Macey thought back to what had been said.

"What are you fucking staring at?" Macey barked.

"I'm not staring. Blimey, keep your hair on."

Macey hated people like this tart. Nosy. "Mind your business. Didn't anyone ever tell you that listening to things that don't concern you only leads to trouble?"

The woman smirked.

"What's so funny?" Macey demanded.

"Nothing."

"Good. Keep it that way."

Macey racked her brain. *Why* had Zoe smirked? Was it the 'trouble' comment? It had to have been. Zoe had known Macey was in the shit because she worked for the fucking *twins*. Macey had been under surveillance and hadn't even known it. *And* Zoe had been there, down the road, after the necklace had been snatched from her. She must have followed Macey then, too. Watched her smugly, knowing she'd be caught, be punished at some point. If Denny hadn't told Macey to meet him later that night, who knew whether she'd be alive today. She didn't even know if she'd be alive tomorrow.

Was she the one in the back of the shop today?

What if George and Greg didn't swallow her story? What if stealing the first necklace was enough reason for them to off her? She could maybe blame that on Denny, make out he'd sent her to Vintage to scope it out before the bigger robbery, but if he was going to be at the warehouse, he'd refute that. She could blag it, couldn't she? Call him a liar to his face? Who were the twins likely to believe, her or a complete scumbag?

"Cat got your tongue?" Moon asked.

"I've been so stupid."

"Yep, and I have to warn you, I think it's too late to make amends. That necklace was worth two grand. That's a lot of money you were prepared to take away from them. People have been sorted for less."

So she was going to die, then. This was her last night, and she was spending it on a hard table, no blanket, no pillow. The Brothers would likely say it was nothing more than she deserved, that *she* was a complete scumbag the same as Denny. Add the second robbery on top, Angie dying, and then there were the refugees, her part in getting them ready to be used and abused. It painted Macey in a terrible light, all of it, not to mention the way she'd spoken about the women to June.

What if June was interrogated and she told them how horrible Macey was? She could lie again, say June was bullshitting, but any number of people would be willing to step forward if asked for a character reference, and they'd all say Macey was someone to steer clear of. There was that lady she'd hit at the sixties disco in the Bassett Hound, all those witnesses…

No, she wasn't getting out of this alive.

Chapter Twenty-Four

Denny got into bed, the alarm on, a gun under his pillow. Patrick had gone to the hospital to sit with Liv and the old dear who hadn't woken up yet. No one had followed them from the party; well, someone *had* been behind, but they'd turned off down a country lane halfway home. Still, he'd be careful. Someone had *known* Macey was at the refugee house, someone had *known* where it was, and he reckoned it was best for him to stay here, out of the way, in case the place got busted. His fingerprints would be there, but he'd say he'd gone there to fuck a woman or two, had paid for the privilege. They couldn't prove he had anything to do with the trafficking business, even if someone dropped his name in it.

Who'd leaked information? Having a mole in the ranks didn't sit well.

He closed his eyes and thought about Oleksiy and Bohuslava. Was it them? Where were they? He hoped they wandered around for hours, tired, and then someone picked them up and raped the cheek out of them. And it was a cheek, running off like that. Who the hell did they think they were?

It annoyed him that all of his threats had fallen on deaf ears. He hadn't been scary enough, or maybe they hadn't understood a word he'd said. Maybe the translator who came whenever the newbies arrived hadn't passed on his exact meaning. Yeah, that was it. Miscommunication, because you could bet, if they'd got the full gist of his threats, they wouldn't have run. He was Denny, someone to pay attention to, and the other women would soon know that come tomorrow. In the morning, he'd type out a statement, put it into Google Translate, and paste it into a document. Print it off. Get them to read it. And watch fear bleed into their faces when they realised the enormity of it all.

He sighed, Macey coming to mind. What was she doing? Spilling all of his secrets? She'd been at the refugee house for long enough to have filed many of them away. She knew how things worked there, the times shit happened, when the women were taken to parties, enough to get The Network in a heap of shit. It was going to come back on him somehow, he knew it. Teo would sack him, call him incompetent because he hadn't captained his ship well enough.

Or kill him.

Ah, bollocks. He'd deal with things as and when. Worrying about it wouldn't solve anything, would it. As his mum used to say, "The problem will still be there even after you've bitten all your nails off, so why bother biting them?" She'd had a few decent sayings, had Mum, and he missed her something chronic. She'd be ashamed of him, though, what he was doing, who he'd become. He hadn't started wheeling and dealing until after his parents had died, couldn't stand to disappoint them while they were alive, suffering instead in that shitty job in that record shop so it looked like he was a good boy. Once they were dead, though, he'd gone for it, and now he wished he hadn't had such high aspirations.

Greedy, that's what he was.

The house alarm blared, startling his eyes open, and he shot out of bed, flinging the pillow away and grabbing the gun, his heart beating double-time. He cocked the weapon, nice and ready so he could fire straight away, and moved across to the door, slowly. He always kept it ajar, the landing light on, but now he wished he'd switched it off. Better to creep about in the dark so whoever had set the alarm going couldn't see him. The trouble with that was, he wouldn't be able to see them either.

He held the gun up in front of him and walked out, whipping into every bedroom, finding them empty. He took the stairs, careful, alert, aiming the gun at the front door. The glass was still intact, so no one had broken it to get inside. He grimaced at the alarm still shrieking, reaching for the keypad and inputting the number to switch it off.

Blessed silence, save for the thud of the pulse in his ears, his harsh breathing.

He entered the living room, elbowing the light switch, the area flooding with brightness. No one greeted him, so with his back to the wall, he sidled down the hallway and into the kitchen. Light on, again no one was there. All that was left was the extension which had his games room one side of the corridor, a dining room on the other, and at the end, a conservatory with his hot tub.

He chose the dining room first. Nothing. No one. Then the games room. It had to have been a cat or something, maybe jumping off the fence onto the conservatory roof. He'd shot a fair few of the little bastards with his BB gun, laughing as they'd run off, screeching. His snooker table, beneath the overhead lights he'd turned on, was the same as always, the balls sitting neatly inside the black plastic triangle.

Hang on. Three were missing.

His skin prickled, and he crouched, checking beneath the table. He stood upright, going behind his well-stocked bar in the corner. The room was empty, but *someone* had been in here, because where were the balls?

He walked out, lungs tightening, and headed down the corridor to the conservatory. Opened the door and stepped over the threshold. It took a split second for him to register that his feet were wet. In the light of the moon streaming through the glass roof, he stared at his hot tub, which was deflating, the pump grunting, letting him know something was wrong. The sides caved in, water gushing, the inflated top sliding to the right. Some bastard had slashed his fucking tub! He sploshed over to the double exit doors. One was ajar, so they'd come in this way. He went outside, the security light splashing on, and waved the gun about. The trees at the bottom of the garden, thick pines, were well able to hide an intruder.

"Who the fuck's there? You'd better piss off, or I'll shoot." He took one step back into the house, then another, the pump squealing now, aggravating his nerves. He closed the door and, too late, spotted the reflection of two men behind him, one of them holding up a sock.

He swung it, and the end connected with the back of Denny's head. The familiar *clack-clack-clack* of snooker balls hitting each other told him where his had gone, and he slipped on the wet floor, screaming, his finger tugging the trigger, a shot firing into the roof and splintering the glass.

He lay there, stunned, and stared up at two faces peering down at him.

"All right, sunshine?" George said, smiling.

Chapter Twenty-Five

Midnight had come and gone. Janine Sheldon stood in the hallway of the refugee house, DS Radburn Linton beside her. A by-the-book Jamaican, he badgered her about her movements sometimes. Okay, most of the time. *Where have you been? Why did you sod off just now? What are you up to?* While his attitude was commendable—every copper should be as honest as the day is long—and he was a good bloke, his interfering got on her last nerve if she was in the process of covering up for the twins. She'd been as honest as him once, and she'd have behaved like him, too, if her senior officer acted shifty, but fucking hell, when it came to sorting out The Brothers' shit, she did *not* need him up her arse.

"So what happened again?" he asked.

She sighed. "Two women ran from a house, got into a taxi, and came to the station. You *know* this."

"So, out in the sticks, there just happened to be a taxi going past, did there? Convenient. Have we chased that up? Checked which company the taxi belongs to or whether it's a sole trader?"

Fucking hell. "There's no information to chase up. I wouldn't imagine for one *second* two frightened captives would have thought to memorise either the taxi number or the bloody licence plate. Would you? Scared for your life, would you *actually* do that?"

"There's CCTV, ANPR."

She didn't need him meddling. "Look, the driver did his job. We don't need to know who he is. If you're trying to say him going past that

244

house is unusual, not really, he could have had a fare that went out of town and he was on his way back. If you think he's suspicious, something to do with the party house—is *that* what you're getting at?—why the hell would he take them to the station, knowing they could get him in trouble? Leave it."

Radburn huffed.

"You can huff all you like," she said, "but we have more important fish to fry, like rounding up everyone in The Network. An innocent taxi driver is plankton compared to the sharks we're after."

She strode upstairs to get away from him, her forensic suit too tight on the wrist and ankle cuffs. There had only been a size small left when she'd snagged it from the back of the SOCO van, and she usually took a medium for comfort. Scenes of Crime were here because of the murder allegation made by Oleksiy and Bohuslava, and officers were doing searches in the woods in the surrounding area, looking for signs the earth had recently been disturbed.

Looking for bodies.

She thought Denny Rawlings was a bit of a dick if he'd ordered the bodies to be buried close by. If it were her, she'd have gone farther afield. He was in the wind, although she'd got word that there had been odd activity at his place. Two uniforms had gone there because his alarm had triggered a response unit, and his hot tub had been slashed, water everywhere. As it had been suspicious, the officers had accessed the house on the 'threat to life' assumption, a break-in gone wrong. A search proved Denny wasn't home but that he'd possibly been to bed because his covers and pillow showed signs of it. He'd likely be at the warehouse, and she could only hope the twins had been their usual diligent selves by wearing their forensic suits, leaving no trace of themselves behind.

The party house had been visited, too, the homeowner, a Mr Johnson, unaware that the women had been part of a sex trafficking operation, or so he'd said. Apparently, he'd ordered the women via a site on the dark web, but digi forensics were on that. People who'd come to the party had long gone. They needed to be traced, spoken to, and it would be a delicate operation because Johnson had confessed it was a sex party, an orgy, basically. Some might not want to admit they'd attended—their spouses wouldn't be best pleased. He hadn't been prepared to give up their names, so it would be old-fashioned detective work in finding them.

Janine didn't hold out much hope.

Of course, Denny hadn't been there either, and Johnson had denied all knowledge of him. That was how outfits like The Network were run. Deny, deny, deny. A twinge of guilt at the waste of resources, the police out there looking for Denny, someone who wouldn't be found, poked Janine. But The Brothers didn't care about such things, budgets, manpower, they expected her to just get on and cover their tracks, lead investigations in the normal manner so no one thought anything was off.

Now, if Radburn would stop his nosing…

She entered a bedroom, the word ONE on the door, and took pity on the women crammed on mattresses. Some appeared scared for their lives; did they think, now the police were here, they'd be sent back home? Did they not know they could seek asylum like every other person fleeing that terrible war? They'd be taken to the station shortly, interpreters provided so they understood it was okay now, they were safe.

"Portland," she said to an officer in protective clothing. "Can I borrow you for an update?"

He came over. "The men Oleksiy mentioned in her statement, Graham and Vincent, aren't here. Most can speak limited English, Oleksiy's been teaching them, but one is better at it and said they're locked in the rooms at night and don't see Graham or Vincent until it's time to go to work again. However…"

"Am I going to like this?"

"Probably not."

"Go on."

"Two men, also missing, stay overnight to watch them. No names have been mentioned, I don't think the fellas ever introduced themselves, but whoever they are, they're young, basically babysitters, and if the women need the toilet, they bang on the floor and one of them unlocks the door and escorts them there."

"Descriptions?"

"One is ginger, the other's a skinhead."

"They could be anyone."

"I know. But for what it's worth, they were kind, never hurt anyone, and the ginger one usually brought bottles of water for them, even though they weren't allowed it."

"Neither Oleksiy nor Bohuslava said a thing about them, but that could come tomorrow. They did say they had other names to drop. Their initial statement was for me to get the state of play, then take them somewhere safe. I'm speaking to them in depth in the morning." She thought about how tired she'd be by then. She'd already been working all day, and it was creeping towards half twelve now. She could assign it to someone else, but she wanted the sisters to feel safe, and they'd already built up a rapport. "So, those two men aren't here either. What does that tell us? They were tipped off?" *By The Brothers?*

"Probably. That's all I've got so far."

She stared at the women. "Have you told them they're not in any trouble and we'll help them?"

"Haven't got round to it yet."

"That should have been the first words out of your mouth. Do it, will you? They look scared to death."

Portland walked over to them and spoke to one who replied in broken English, then she related what he'd said.

Their faces changed. Smiles. Shoulders relaxing. Tears.

Jesus Christ, those poor cows.

The emotion emanating from them was so strong Janine had to leave the room.

She joined DI Keith Sykes in a second bedroom, an empty one, as the women had been shepherded into ONE to keep them all together while transport was being arranged. He inspected the bedding, perhaps seeing something of significance, or hoping he would.

The operation was too big for her to run it by herself, and while she was the SIO and appreciated the help, it gave her a headache as she couldn't keep track of what Keith was doing when she was elsewhere. He could action shit without telling her first. She'd sort that now so he knew the score.

"Run everything by me," she said. "I want to be in the loop on absolutely everything."

"What if I need to action something as a matter of importance? I can't be phoning you if, say, we find a body in the loft, the garden or whatever, to ask if I can proceed."

"I don't mean that kind of thing, I mean keep me up to date so I can assess accordingly. If you find a body, you phone me, simple as that."

"Right."

"Something interesting I noticed… You were waiting here from eleven-thirty, just before the women were brought back. Where were the police vehicles positioned?"

"We parked them in the field opposite the property, behind some trees."

"There are what, about twelve women? How were they dropped off? Cars?"

"A minibus."

"And where is that now?"

"Officers are looking for it. By the time we arrived on foot, they'd been locked in the house and the minibus had driven off."

That didn't add up. She calculated the distance from the field to the house, plus the time frame. "Wasn't anyone actioned to wait in cars down the main road, left and right, just in case?"

"We weren't expecting the bus to fuck off."

We? *He'd* been in charge of this part of the operation, not anyone else. "But *you* should have anticipated it as the lead at this scene. Were any officers out the back?"

"No."

What the fuck? "Um, why? It's standard bloody procedure!"

"We thought—*I* thought—it'd be a case of getting across the road, running up the drive, and apprehending the men."

She frowned, feeling like Radburn—nosy, checking, poking her hooter in—but something was well off here. Had she recognised Keith was acting dodgy because *she* was dodgy? "While I appreciate you had a lot on your mind, the time it would have taken to scoot across the road, up the drive, compared to the time it would take for the men to deliver the women and lock them in the rooms…they're about the same, yes?"

"Maybe."

"So when the men walked out of the house, you and your team would have been at the front door, right?"

His blush crept over the top of his mask. "It didn't work out like that."

"Clearly. So how *did* it work out?"

"Err, we were only halfway up the drive when they got back in the minibus and drove past us."

"Oh right. Just imagine if you'd had officers hiding out the back, eh? You could have contacted them to get to the front door and apprehend them. Amazing, that sort of police work. I'm giving you fair warning, someone is going to spot the errors like I did and poke into it."

"Sorry, all right? It was all a bit of a panic."

"I don't see why it would be. We knew in advance the average time the women would arrive. You and your team were here, waiting. I'm thinking you waited a little too long to give the word to approach the house. As soon as they'd turned into the driveway, you should have run. When *did* you give the word?"

"Once they went inside. I wanted it so they were indoors and had less chance of legging it across the fields."

"Wow. So let's go with this scenario. You could have approached and entered through the already busted front door. They could have fled out the back way, and as there were *no officers to stop them*, they'd have hightailed it over a field, getting away, so your claim of there being less chance of escape is a load of codswallop."

"I fucked up."

"It looks that way, but it *also* looks like you engineered it to give the men time to leave. No cars on the road to block their way. What about the other two missing men?"

"What men?"

"There are usually babysitters here."

He frowned. "No one was here but the women."

She lowered her voice, her next words a test, to flush him out if he wasn't on the level. "If you're going to play at being a bent copper, you need to up your game, mate."

His eyes narrowed. "I don't know what you're on about."

"Don't you? It'll be looked into, you know that, don't you. Every one of your movements will be picked over because the men got away and our seniors will want to know why. Your team will be questioned…" She shook her head. "If you're involved in this, you'd better be prepared to lie out of your arse and come out smelling of roses."

"Why are you saying all this?" he whispered. "Why the friendly warning?"

Because I might need you to cover my back in the future, and if I've got something on you, you can't use whatever I do against me. "Because I know how, sometimes, we get ourselves into situations we wish we hadn't. Sort it. Make sure you keep your nose clean from here on out. Sex with refugees isn't worth the fallout, understand? That *is* why you were paying particular attention to that

254

bedding just now, wasn't it? Has it got your semen on it? Dear God, you'd better hope not. And if you're part of The Network, God fucking help you, because I can't."

He nodded, confirming her assessment. "I don't know what to say."

"Thank you?" Why was she teaching him how to game the system? Yes, she could use him later down the line, but shouldn't she be disgusted if he was a part of The Network? Shouldn't she want him arrested? Probably, but he was a damn good copper… Did he deserve a second chance? "Listen, if you're involved with this in the way I'm thinking, *don't* pass on to them how the investigation is proceeding. Learn when to hedge your bets. Step back, say you're being watched. Distance yourself."

"You should be cuffing me."

"I should, but you've got kids, yes? A wife?"

"You know I do."

"Then think of them instead of your dick or how full your pockets are with the cash you're probably paid. Think of how any leaders who get wind of this will act towards you."

"Are you saying you're involved with The Br—"

"I'm saying nothing of the sort. One chance, one pass, got it? I'll be watching you."

Movement out on the landing had them both glancing that way. Thank fuck for masks, because they hid their undoubtedly guilty expressions. An officer studied the banisters, hopefully unaware of what they'd been discussing.

Janine went into professional mode. "I'll leave this scene to you, Keith. I'm going to take Radburn to the closest woods and oversee things there, then we'll visit the other sites. After that, we'll be at the station if you need me. I want to check on the progress in finding members of The Network. It's going to be an all-nighter." She paused. "Are you okay with all that?"

"Yep."

"The DCI is dealing with The Network side of things, so hopefully he'll have something to tell me by the time we get there." She glared to get her point across: *we're in this together now*. "I'll let you know if there's anything *significant* you need to be aware of."

"Cheers."

"Okay, I'll leave you be. Of course, I'll message you with any other developments, and you do the same for me."

"Will do."

She left the room, going over why she'd handed him an escape route when he'd been involved in some way, abusing women. Whether it was having sex with them as a customer or he was in deep with The Network, he was still a party to their suffering. It was for purely selfish reasons. Without him realising it, she could use him when she had to help the twins. He'd be handy when having to look things up on the database so her name wasn't associated with it.

She joined Radburn in the living room. "Anything to report?"

"A load of fingerprints, the usual."

"Good. Let's hope they match people in the system. I'm specifically interested in men called Graham and Vincent, plus two unknowns who babysat the women overnight." She had to get hold of the twins. "I need some air."

"You always do." Radburn eyed her funny.

"You seem to *really* have a problem with the fact that I need a moment to myself at scenes to process the shit I've seen and heard. It's called getting a grip when the horror of it takes hold. It's called taking a few to centre yourself so you can dig deep and return to the scene and behave in a competent manner. If that offends you, tough tits. We're going to visit the various woods locations next, so meet me at the car in five."

She stalked to the back door, took her protectives off and popped them in a bag, then placed new shoe covers on to fuck off to the bottom of the garden and use her burner phone.

JANINE: IS THERE SOMETHING I NEED TO KNOW? FOUR MEN ARE BEING LOOKED FOR. GRAHAM AND VINCENT, DON'T KNOW THEIR SURNAMES, AND TWO OTHERS WHO SHOULD HAVE BEEN AT THE REFUGEE HOUSE FOR WHEN THE WOMEN CAME BACK. OVERNIGHT BABYSITTERS. DO YOU HAPPEN TO KNOW WHY THEY'RE NOT HERE? DON'T PHONE ME, I'M AT A SCENE.

GG: NO IDEA WHO G AND V ARE, BUT THE OTHER TWO... ONE IS OUR INFORMANT, THE OTHER IS HIS COLLEAGUE. BOTH VACATED AFTER MOON ET AL WENT THERE TO COLLECT A CERTAIN PERSON.

JANINE: WHAT CERTAIN PERSON?

GG: DOESN'T MATTER. SHE'LL BE GONE BY MORNING.

JANINE: FUCK'S SAKE. THE INFORMANT... ANY CHANCE THEIR FINGERPRINTS ARE GOING TO BE FLAGGED?

258

GG: Unsure if he's been arrested in the past. Hang on while I ask. I'll also ask about G and V.

She paced, deleting the message string, glancing at the house. Radburn came out, sorted his protectives, then stomped round the front. She'd pissed him off but didn't care. He'd get over his grump at some point.

Her phone blipped.

GG: He's clean, as is his mate.

Janine: That's one thing off my plate, then. What about G and V?

GG: They're just drivers. My mole doesn't know if they've been in the shit with you lot.

Janine: Then if they're caught, he'd better hope they don't mention who he is.

GG: Doesn't matter if they do. He uses a nickname. Any news on who killed Angie yet?

Janine: No, although the blue sports car was found earlier. Registered to Denny, so that's another reason to haul him in.

GG: What a bloody prick.

Janine: Got to go. Bodies to find.

GG: Enjoy!

She smiled, despite trying not to. It had to be George she'd spoken to. His dry humour gave him away.

She shoved her phone in her pocket and walked down to where she'd parked on the road. A PC stood at a cordon strung up across the mouth of the drive, and she popped her shoe covers in the bag he held up, then signed out of the log, dipped beneath the tape, and strode to her car.

Radburn was on the phone, and her heart lurched at the thought of him sending a message to someone, saying Janine was possibly bent. As she'd thought before, she thought it again now: she needed him moved off her team but had to think of a decent enough excuse to get rid of him. Maybe she could play it that he was so good at questioning things, he'd be better suited in a taskforce that would benefit from his dogged determination. *He's wasted on my team, sir. Think of how well he'd do under DCI Fletcher, sir…*

Hmm.

She got in the car, relieved to find he played a game, linking rows of fruit. "Having a moment to process, are you?" A dig, but she couldn't help it.

"I get it now, all right? Didn't realise I nipped a quick game in when things were getting to me."

"Glad we're on the same page."

She started the engine. "I've been thinking… What's your endgame?"

She drove in the direction of the first potential deposition site—she'd called it deposition, but it may well be where some of the murders had taken place. Oleksiy had told her the women had been killed at the house, though, then taken to the woods, but it didn't mean she'd witnessed all of them.

"What do you mean?" He shut his phone off.

"What do you want to achieve in your job? How many rungs do you want to climb?"

"I don't want to be DCI or a super, if that's what you mean."

"What are you after, then?"

"I like being in the thick of it. Working things out."

She remembered what she'd so recently thought of saying to her boss. "You're wasted on my team, you know that, don't you."

"What?"

"You're too good. Ever thought about transferring to something like Serious Crimes?

The NCA? You'd suit an intelligence role rather than traipsing around with me."

"D'you think so?"

"I wouldn't have said if I didn't. Have a think about it. I'll put in a good word for you." She prayed he took the bait and she was assigned a less intrusive DS next time round. Someone lazy would be ideal, who didn't care where she was or what she was doing. "Okay, we're here. Deep breath."

They left the car and approached the cordon attached to two trees, signing the log then putting on protectives. She was thankful there was a medium size here.

"Who's the scene manager?" she asked the PC.

"Sheila Sutton."

Oh good. Janine liked her. "Where is she?"

"A shout went up about ten minutes ago, so she'll be farther in."

Janine gritted here teeth. As SIO, she expected to have been alerted about the shout, but maybe Sheila was making sure it was a body first. "Thanks."

She led the way into the woods. Light to the left guided her, and she came upon a group of officers standing beneath a halogen, Sheila with them, staring at the ground. Oh God, was that a *hand* poking through the mud? The mound of earth hadn't even been packed down, it was loose, and didn't appear to have been covered with forest debris. Why hadn't the site been disguised? Had Denny sent his men to bury that poor woman and hadn't given them proper instructions? If he had, they'd ignored him.

Bunch of novices.

"Ah, Janine," Sheila said. "I was just about to phone you."

Janine sighed. "A fresh one by the looks of it."

"Hmm." Sheila held her mobile up. "I'll phone in and get the ball rolling."

Chapter Twenty-Six

*T*he first threat of murder came a few months after they'd arrived. They'd been moved to another room, TWO on the door, and new women had come to fill ONE. Not all of the women, though. Three were missing: Daryna, Anhelina, and Mykhaila. Oleksiy had overheard Denny telling someone they were being killed, taken to the woods. Buried.

"They're going to kill them," she whispered close to Bohuslava's ear on their new mattress. "Shh, don't say anything to the others. They don't need to know."

"I don't need to know either. Why are you telling me?"

"So I build your trust again. Everything I hear, I'll pass to you."

"О, Боже."

"Don't say that, they'll know something's wrong."

"Everyone says it. We're always fucking saying it."

The sound of the lock being disengaged had everyone waking and sitting upright, gasps going round, a shriek or two, although they were muted. Denny had said they had to shut up as their noises got on his nerves. He came in followed by Patrick, the gunman, and a naked Anhelina who'd been crying. She shivered, her hands bound in front of her with rope. The interpreter entered, smiling, the hateful bastard.

Denny shut the door. Locked it. "You three, get off that mattress and out of the way."

The trio in the top-left corner scrabbled to do as they'd been told, camping out on other mattresses, squeezed between the current occupants. Patrick shoved Anhelina onto the vacated space. She bounced, banging her head on the wall, and he got on there, straddling her. She brought her joined hands up to hide her face, hide her ugly crying. Oleksiy stared around at everyone, scared to death because she knew this wasn't going to be sexual abuse this time like the day they'd first arrived. Bohuslava knew, too, and she looked as if she wanted to spit at Patrick, to get up and protect Anhelina, but if she did, if any of them did, they'd be killed, too.

"Now then, if you don't make the grade, if you don't perform well, we don't need you anymore, boss' orders." Denny pointed at Anhelina while the interpreter passed on what he'd said. "She was all right at first, a bit skittish, although the punters expect that with a new batch. But by now she should be at least pretending she's enjoying it, know what I mean?"

Everyone stared at the interpreter.

"You all know," Denny went on, "that by the end of your six-month probation period, you should be acting like proper sex workers. In order to live, you need to behave like you know what you're doing. People don't want to fuck mannequins, they want to be desired. Pretend if you don't like it, otherwise, this is what's going to happen to you."

Patrick wrenched Anhelina's hands away from her face and clamped his around her neck. And squeezed.

267

She let out a garbled sound, her eyes bugging, and she tried to kick him with her knees. Raise her hands to push his from the undersides. Nothing worked, he kept on squeezing, arms straight, focus immense. He stared into her eyes for what seemed like forever—a few minutes must have passed with some looking away because they couldn't stand it, or others, like Oleksiy and Bohuslava, watching everything so they could remember it if they ever felt the need to not perform properly. A reminder of what they'd go through.

He let go eventually, checking for a pulse casually, then stood beside the interpreter, both of them with erections. Denny didn't have one, so at least he didn't get off on death and violence, nor did he become aroused at seeing them all naked.

"Did you get the message?" he said. "She'll be taken to the woods, buried." He smiled. "Don't get too relaxed. You've got to watch the other two being offed yet."

He unlocked the door, and Patrick dragged Anhelina off the mattress and across the floor, her black hair the last thing to disappear through the doorway. Amid quiet whimpers, Oleksiy struggled to hold down vomit. She'd just watched a murder, seen the moment the life had left a woman's eyes, and she'd be haunted by it forever.

She vowed to escape, to bring Denny and everyone here down, although not the two young men who came up during the night to let them go to the bathroom. One of them brought bottles of water, something that wasn't allowed, and he always looked at her respectfully, in the eyes, not at her tits or other private areas.

Mykhaila was brought in, shrieking—she must have seen Anhelina being dragged down the landing—and the awful scenario played out again. And with Daryna.

"Remember," Denny said when it was over, "if you want to end up like them, do a crap job. If not, spread your legs wider and smile."

Chapter Twenty-Seven

The morning had dawned bright, birds chirping like loons, a slight nip in the air that would burn off once the sun got its head in the game. A few crocuses had sprung up in the twins' front garden, some white, some purple, and George couldn't recall planting the fuckers. Maybe Greg had arranged that. George had plucked a lilac-coloured one, popped it in his suit lapel, and the scent of it wafted up as he perused the tools on the table in the warehouse.

Denny had been hanging on the rack all night, babysat by Martin who didn't like getting involved in the gory stuff. He'd gone now, off to collect some protection money, preferring that job over any other. He'd kipped on the sofa, pulling the bed section out, and said Denny had slept throughout, Martin having administered an injection provided by their dodgy doctor, to knock him out.

Denny currently sat on the wooden chair, awake, naked, held in place by the usual ropes. He had an egg-sized lump on his head from where George had walloped him with the snooker-ball sock. Denny had protested his innocence as soon as he'd woken up.

George had said, "If you're not involved, why bring The Network up? Most people wouldn't have a clue what that is, yet you're bleating on about it."

The stupid prick had realised his mistake and clamped his lips shut.

Macey sat beside him on a foldout chair, also naked, also roped up. She looked like she'd slept rough, and George supposed she had, considering she'd spent the night on Moon's torture table. When they'd collected her earlier, Moon had passed on the information she'd given him, and while she seemed to have realised the error of her ways, George didn't give a single fuck. She hadn't cared when she'd robbed that necklace from Vintage the first time and she hadn't cared about going back with that Honda fella either.

George personally thought she was a bit of a dickhead—she'd had a phone at the refugee house, one that Moon had switched off and thrown out of the window on their way to the air-raid shelter—and despite her claim that Denny was scary, surely she had *someone* she could have contacted for help. At the point Denny had first taken her to the refugee house, all she'd done was nick a necklace. He'd had nothing else on her. Why then, had she stayed there and gone ahead with the second robbery? George knew full well why. It wasn't because she'd been forced or frightened into it. She'd had her beady eye on a big payout.

No, she didn't deserve their sympathy, nor any leniency.

George turned from the tool table, a weapon in hand, to find Greg standing in front of the stupid pair. His brother stared as if his eyes had gone glassy and he wasn't really seeing them. What was he thinking? Did he wonder about Ruffian and whether George was going to let him out? No, George couldn't do that. Ruffian was for when he worked alone. Mad George would be the one to deal with Denny and Macey, although he didn't feel Mad waiting to arrive, so maybe he'd have to get this done as his usual self.

George clicked his fingers in front of Greg's face. "Where did you go?"

Greg shook his head. "Doesn't matter. Right, are you doing this or do you want my help?"

"Depends how you're feeling. You lost focus just now…"

Greg sniffed. "I'll go and play the Xbox, then."

He'd got into it through Martin and Will. While Greg booted the system up, *Call of Duty* appearing on the bigger flatscreen they'd installed last week, George slapped a crowbar on his palm. Since becoming Ruffian—before that, to be fair—he'd grown bored with this scenario. Thinking up different ways to kill someone to assuage Mad George's penchant for kills to be fresh and novel was now annoying. With Ruffian, he had spontaneity, creeping up on victims, allowing things to go whichever way they would. A surprise, not knowing what he'd do next. A big contrast to how he'd always been, needing to be in control at all times. He'd learnt to let go a little, to embrace change, and to be honest, he fucking well enjoyed it.

Today, he wanted answers from Denny so he could pass them on to Janine, and he wanted to watch Macey try to get herself out of the shit, for his amusement only. Other than that, a few wallops with the crowbar along the way, he'd likely give them a quick kill. Later, he'd go out as Ruffian and see where that led him.

"I'll talk to you first," he said to Denny. "Come on then, give me your cock-and-bull story. I may as well get a laugh out of your lies."

Denny spat at George's feet. "*I* should be the one standing where you are."

"What do you mean?"

"It doesn't matter now, does it, because I'm not going to get what I want." Denny rubbed his head lump and winced, bringing his hand down to stare at the blood on his fingertips.

"Forgot to tell you, the pressure in that lump split the skin a bit more just before you woke up. And the reason you woke up so abruptly was I poured TCP on it to get a reaction."

"I gather that, I can fucking smell it."

"For someone who should be watching what he says, you're doing a piss-poor job of it."

"Why should I watch what I say? You're going to kill me, aren't you?"

"Yeah, but I expected you to beg for forgiveness or something. Most people do. You know, a last-ditch effort to get me to go easy."

"You're not known for that, so it'd be pointless me trying." Denny smiled, and it wasn't pleasant. Something was going on inside his head to draw out such an arrogant expression.

George sighed. "Say what you've got to say. I'll indulge you."

"I was going to take the estate."

George roared with laughter. "Were you now. And how were you going to do that?"

"Dunno, hadn't got round to making the final plans."

"Too busy with the refugees?"

"Something like that. But I'd have done it. I'd have killed you two."

"Aren't you aware of the way leadership works, then? Someone's already in the wings to take our place if we get killed. You might have managed to rule for a day or so, but you'd have been taken out unless you had a strong army behind you."

"Whatever."

"Bless you, silly boy, thinking it would be simple." George swung the crowbar, and it connected with Denny's shin.

The bloke screamed, and Macey flinched, leaning away from him as if his pain was contagious and might infect her any second if she breathed it in. Denny gritted his teeth, keening, and George stared at the gorgeous sight of ragged bone poking through the torn and bruised skin. Only a bit, but it pleased him it had broken and would be giving Denny endless amounts of gyp.

"Calm down, sunshine, that's just the beginning." George smiled.

Denny attempted to control himself, eyes closed, teeth gritted, whimpers seeping around them. His skin flushed from the agony, then the redness disappeared, leaving him pale and sweaty, gasping, his shoulders rising with each inhale.

"That's for thinking you could take Cardigan off us." George paused until Denny shut up. "Now then, let's move on to the robbery. Your sports car's been picked up by the police, just so you know, so they'd have come after you for sending Honda and this silly cow here to Vintage. That would have been a better thing for you, getting nicked, spending the rest of your life in prison, but I'm not about what's best for scum. I'm about what's best for me and my brother and those poor women. It's obvious why you chose Vintage, the jewellery in that haul is worth thirty grand, but what I want to know is, why did you send Macey in when you already had Honda?"

"That's what I want to know," Macey muttered.

George pointed the crowbar at her. "Shut your cakehole, it's not your turn to speak yet." He switched his gaze to Denny. "Come on then, let's have it, son."

"Don't call me son," Denny snapped.

"I'll call you what I fucking like, pickle. I mean, it's not like you can do anything about it, is it, considering your current predicament." George laughed. Some people were such *dickheads*, full of their own self-importance. He ignored the fact he felt the same way—after all, he had the chops to back his words up, unlike Denny.

The plonker sighed. "I used her because I could. Because she got shitty with me when she tried to flog me that necklace. I didn't like it. She needed to learn a lesson."

"Ah. Right. So you didn't like her talking to you in a certain way and felt she should pay for it by being put in the frame for murder. Hmm, interesting, except for the fact your car was seen leaving the scene with Macey and Honda in it. Honestly, mistakes like that can cost you your life, as you've found out."

"Fuck off. Like you've never made a mistake before."

"Oh, I have, but I tend not to make them twice if I can help it. That's two times your car's been connected to Vintage robberies." George thought of Janet and cringed—she was an error on his part, but he aimed to fix that. "I always have a backup plan, a way to cover my mistakes. Why did Honda kill Angie? Did you tell him to?"

"Yep." Denny brightened at that.

The fucker was *chuffed* she'd died?

Denny continued, "To keep *her* in line." He jerked his lumpy head towards Macey.

"You must have had something else in mind to have kept her at the refugee house other than doing a bit of makeup."

"I was going to turn her into a sex slave."

"You what?" Macey screeched. "You absolute bastard!"

George shouted, "I said, shut your cakehole! Fuck me, your voice is like nails on a chalkboard. Be. *Quiet*." He stared at her, wanting to punch her lights out, gripping the crowbar instead and smacking it onto Denny's shrivelled-from-fear wedding tackle.

Another scream, eyes scrunched shut, knees drawn up, big toes pushing into the floor. Tears seeping. Spit dribbling.

Fucker.

George waited for the noise to stop. Macey stared at Denny's private parts, eyes wide at the sight of his testicles swelling, the skin coated with an angry purple bruise. George bent to sniff the crocus in his lapel as piss squirted from Denny's cock, gathered in a river where his thighs met, then dripped over, down his shins, on that wound, and onto the floor.

George grinned. "Two more discussions to clear things up, two more wallops, then it'll all be over. Can't say fairer than that, can I. Right, Denny, if you'd just stop moaning, I'll be your best friend forever." He waited. Waited. Fucking *waited*. "That's better. The Network. What's that all about?"

"It's obvious."

"So you're happy to work for someone who takes advantage of women running from a *war* zone? You don't even need to answer that. What kind of bastard *are* you?"

"I wanted money. Needed it behind me so I could take over Cardigan."

George chuckled. "I still find it funny how you can even think you'd have been able to do that. Denny Rawlings, some prick who steals and makes out he gives to charity."

"That's where you're wrong. That's not just who I am. I'm someone else. Bigger, stronger. That Denny is who I *wanted* people to see. I played a part so no one would ever dream I'd have the balls to snatch Cardigan, then when they realised what I'd done, they'd see I was so much more."

George didn't like the comparison. *He* was different people, too. "But people would have laughed their arses off at you. *That* Denny, playing at being a leader? Fuck me, you'd have been roasted by everyone."

"I just said they'd have realised I wasn't really that side of me, didn't I? Jesus, talk about not listening."

"Oh, I'm listening, but *you're* not. People know you as that Denny, and even if you showed them a different side, it'd take some work to convince them you're not an incompetent prick—which you are, we've established that by you letting Honda use your car."

"You don't understand."

George shrugged. "Who's the big boss?"

"I don't know his name."

"You're lying."

"So what if I am? It's not like you're going to let me walk free if I tell you, is it, so what's the point?"

"So true." George let loose with the crowbar again, this time on a knee.

That scream reverberated through his veins.

Nice.

Chapter Twenty-Eight

Denny couldn't hack this anymore. The pain was unbearable. Yeah, he knew there were worse pains out there, George might well inflict it on him soon, but at this moment, when his world had turned black, and white noise thrummed in his ears, it was about as much as he could handle. Anything more, and he'd black out. Maybe that was for the best. Maybe he should just let the darkness claim him and be done with it. At least he wouldn't feel the agony of dying then.

But a part of him still had hope. Stupid of him? Yeah, but they said that, didn't they, that when you faced the end of your life, unless you were tired of living, you strived to stay alive. Instinct, wasn't it, to fight? A voice whispered that he was an asset if George would only stop and think about it. Denny could be good for The Brothers, be someone they could use to run Cardigan. Another voice whispered that he'd royally fucked up by telling him he wanted their estate, so there was no way George would trust him now anyway.

Why didn't Denny think before he spoke? Why didn't he think before he acted? That jibe about letting Honda use his car had been a valid one. He should have insisted on a stolen one, false number plates. Honda had ditched it; the police had found it. Of course they'd have been looking for Denny. Good job he'd been at the refugee house all day, then. If he could get hold of Honda now…

"You went quiet quickly this time." George slapped the crowbar on his palm again.

The action had got on Denny's nerves the first time, so *this* time? If he wasn't tied with rope, and despite his injuries, he'd have got up and snatched that bar and caved George's head in with it. Yeah, Greg would have killed him once he'd realised, although saying that, he had big headphones on and played a game, so Denny could have walked up behind him, whacked him one, then turned on Macey and killed her an' all. Fucking slag.

"Where does Honda live?" George asked.

"Fuck you." Although Denny *should* tell him, considering Honda had dumped the car instead of bringing it back to the refugee house, the prick. Why protect him now? If the police picked Honda up and he told them Denny had organised the Vintage robbery and belonged to The Network, so what? They couldn't do anything to him now because he wouldn't exist soon. As for Macey, if Honda mentioned her name, that didn't matter either, because she was going to Hell right alongside Denny. There was no way George was letting her off the hook.

"Shame you don't want to play ball."

George sniffed a flower in his lapel, had his nose right in the petals, the fucking insane weirdo. Christ.

"Fuck this." Denny might as well blab. He was fucked now, the struck parts of him throbbing and aching, the lump on his head seeming to expand. He gave the address. "If Honda's not there, try the Bassett Hound."

George raised his eyebrows. "Oh, I know that place. We were there not long ago. Nice gaff. The landlord's on our payroll."

Denny hadn't known that. Hang on, *what* did he just say? "Patrick?"

"Yeah. Know him, do you?"

"You could say that." *Did he grass me up? Has he been spying all this time?* "What did he have to say for himself, then?"

"Nothing to do with you. All he would say was that Macey had been in a few days ago and got thrown out."

"Since when's he been working for you?"

"We informed yesterday. People don't have a choice if we choose them. Why does it matter so much to you?"

"It doesn't."

If it was only yesterday, is that why Patrick wanted to be called by his Minion name? Shall I tell George he works for The Network?

Denny imagined Patrick being slaughtered, and while he was pissed off his right-hand man had been roped into the twins' web, Patrick wouldn't have had a say in it. Fuck, none of it mattered anymore.

George raised the crowbar, and Denny braced himself for impact. The weapon seemed to move in slow motion. Gone were his dreams of ruling the estate, people looking up to him, *fearing* him. Gone was him modelling himself even more on Teo. His house came to mind, how it used to be when he'd been a kid, Mum and Dad so proud of it. Good people, they'd never put a foot wrong intentionally, and they'd be in Heaven now, so far away from where he was going, down into Hell.

"Sorry," he whispered to them, then the bar struck.

Chapter Twenty-Nine

Macey screamed at the sight of the bar cleaving Denny's skull. Blood spattered onto her shoulder, her cheek. Hot, horrible, going cold quickly. The weapon got stuck, George attempting to wrench it out, in the end having to put his foot on the ropes around Denny's stomach and tugging hard.

George was a monster, a fucking *monster*, and she stood no chance of escaping the same fate.

Horrified, she stared at him poking the straight end of the crowbar into the hole in Denny's head, pushing it deeper into his brain. Blood pooled in the dent George had made, dripping into Denny's hair, down his forehead, and splashing onto his wrecked nuts. Macey's body was colder than she'd ever been, as if ice filled her from the inside, locking her immobile, her teeth chattering. She went to stop screaming then realised she already had, her voice as frozen as everything else. Time stilled, that crowbar poking out of the head, George's hand on the other end, then it sped up. The bar came out, castoff spray arcing, and George threw it on the floor, the clang loud, infiltrating her ears, her head, echoing.

George walked behind her, and she shit herself, thinking he was going to get another tool and hurt her with it, but he gripped the back of Denny's chair and dragged him away. Macey didn't dare turn her head to see where he'd gone. She grabbed the chance to compose herself, to will heat into her body to thaw it so she could speak when he interrogated her, which he would, wouldn't he? Or had he taken what she'd said to

Moon last night as her explanation and planned to kill her fast now, bored already with this situation?

He appeared again, nothing but a phone in hand, and typed out a message. "Just letting our copper know the score," he said to her casually, as if what he'd just done was of no consequence.

She couldn't get over his calmness, his…was professionalism the right word? This must be child's play to him. He probably did this day in, day out. She'd heard about the Wilkes' rise into gang life, how as teenagers they'd started working for Ron Cardigan, then when he'd died, they'd taken over. What George had said to Denny about leaders waiting in the wings was a lie. *They'd* stepped in and maintained control of the estate, so Denny would have been able to as well. Or maybe the twins had been the ones in the wings all along.

It didn't matter. What did, was George being so adept at what he did. Not a speck of sympathy had been in his eyes when he'd dealt with Denny, more like mocking, thinking Denny was shit on his shoe. And look at Greg, playing a fucking *game* as if none of this was happening. The pair of them were mental, had to be. Rumour said they were, stories had gone around of how they acted, but to actually see it for herself had been frightening. This was so much worse than anything on the telly, and she'd come to the realisation that she'd been naïve, utterly *stupid* to think she could talk this man round. He wasn't going to accept the sob story she'd cooked up during the night, no way, but she'd fight for her life, her freedom, until the end. Tell him anyway.

"All done," George said. "She's going to hold off going after Honda. He's ours. Can't say I blame her, she's up to her armpits in it at the moment."

Macey pitied the bloke, even though he'd been a bastard and killed Angie. She pitied anyone who was brought here and had to suffer George's wrath.

"Let's have *our* little chat now, shall we?" His suit had blood on it, and his face was covered in red freckles. He fiddled with the knot of his scarlet tie. "We'll go from the beginning. Why did you take the necklace?"

Here was the sob story, all lies. "I grew up poor. Like, proper poor. Hungry all the time, my clothes either too big or too small, all from the charity shops. They weren't washed, I stank, I didn't have much food, and in the end, the social took me off my mum and dad. They're dead now, thank fuck. I was put into care, moved from place to place, all the foster people touching me up, you know, abusing me. When I was old enough to leave, they'd found me this shitty bedsit. There was a bloke in there, he raped me every Saturday night when he was drunk and—"

"What a load of old cobblers." George smiled. "Nice try, but in the time since you nicked that necklace, we've been looking for you. Looking *into* you. Your mum and dad live in Essex now— pretty cottage, all that ivy on it. Before they relocated there, you lived with them on Cardigan until you were twenty-one, then you moved into the place you currently live. I suspect, with what you've just said, you were then going to say you had to turn to robbing to survive, that it was the only way you could feed yourself and pay the rent, when everyone knows you're a fucking klepto who can't be arsed to get a proper job. Try again. Why did you nick the necklace?"

Shit. "Because it's what I do. I wanted a break, needed a chunk of money so I didn't have to keep pinching clothes and selling them on for a bit. The shops were getting wise to me, even the ones Up West."

"So you said to yourself, 'I know, I'll rob The Brothers, what a *great* idea!'"

"I didn't know you'd bought it. I thought Angie had."

"Yet somewhere along the way, you must have found out we owned it, but you were still prepared to go in there with Honda. What bullshit's going to come out of your mouth next? Let me guess. Denny forced you to do it."

"He *did*! That bit's the God's honest, I swear. He picked me up on the day I stole the necklace. I met him at night. He took me to that fucking house, said I had to do the robbery and the makeup for the women."

"Why didn't you ring for help?"

"Because I've *got* no one who'd help me, that's why, plus he scared me."

"You could have phoned your parents. The police. Even the pigs are better than being with Denny. A stint in the nick for a little robbery would have given you the break you wanted."

"You wouldn't understand."

"I understand all right. You wanted part of the spoils from the Vintage robbery. You'd forgo the grand you were asking for the necklace if it meant you'd get more." He paused to sniff the flower. "Lovely. Shame they don't do aftershave with that smell."

She stared at him. He went from frightening to normal in an instant.

"I watched the CCTV footage," he said. "You were smiling at one point. If you were so scared, if you didn't want to be there, why would you get enjoyment out of it?"

"Again, you wouldn't understand."

"Not really sure I want to. I'm only asking these questions to string it out so you're sitting there wondering when I'm going to strike and what with. The crowbar's on the floor, so hmm, what have I got up my sleeve?"

Her innards seemed to bounce around, and she felt sick.

"Also on CCTV, it seemed to me you hadn't expected Honda to slit Angie's throat. You were scared, weren't you? Shocked. I imagine it was a lot to take in, seeing her like that. Did you scream, is that why you had your mouth open?"

"I couldn't…I couldn't even scream. It was too horrible."

"You screamed without much trouble when I staved Denny's head in. Did you keep quiet in the shop because you were afraid someone would hear you and catch you there? Conversely, did you scream here because you hoped someone outside *would* hear you and come to your rescue? No point, the place is soundproofed, so make all the racket you like."

He paced for a bit. Sniffed the flower. Paced. He was so *weird*, so hard to make out. Apart from the blood on him, he looked like any other person, waiting for a bus, say, contemplating life, thinking nice things. His outer façade was so carefully honed—he had immense control, he wasn't fazed by her or what he planned to do to her. It was as if this was *boring*.

He stopped. Cocked his head at her. "D'you know, I think I've had enough of you now. I won't kill you yet, though. I've got work to do with Denny, then I'll come to you. Sit tight, don't go anywhere."

He roared with laughter, and she followed him with her eyes. He wandered off through a doorway. While he was gone, she stared at the back of Greg's head, then at the screen where bullets blasted people to death and bodies flew to the ground. She wished that would happen to her, a quick bullet, then she'd be gone.

The *schlep* sound of the door opening had her looking that way. George appeared in a forensics suit, and she idly wondered whether his copper had given it to him. He had the hood up—the elastic edges dug into his face—and gloves, booties. He bent to untie a dead Denny and dragged him across the floor to place him in front of that creepy rack on the wall. He positioned him into a star shape, tilted his head as if checking he'd done it just so. Disappearing behind her for a second or two, he came back holding a circular saw which he fired up, the noise it generated setting Macey's teeth on edge. He bent over at Denny's feet and chopped one off, placing it sole down, then proceeded to slice off the toes and the rest of the foot in two-inch slabs. He sang 'My Old Man's a Dustman' while he was at it, and she gawped, revolted, amazed by his blasé attitude. Who sang while sawing people up? Who *did* that?

This was him showing her what was coming her way, she wasn't stupid, she knew that well enough, and thoughts she shouldn't be thinking, things she shouldn't even *care* about, entered her mind. He'd see her, every part of her, and could laugh at her dimpled bum and going-saggy tits. He'd view all the parts of herself she hated, parts she didn't want anyone else to see. Yes, she was naked now, but the rope hid a chunk of her, gave her the feeling she wasn't so exposed, but down there, on the floor, her arms and legs splayed... Her vanity was irrelevant against dying, wasn't it? The mortification paled into insignificance when confronted with not knowing the manner of death, how much pain she'd be in, how she might end up begging to die because the agony was too much.

It took a while for him to finish. With Denny in pieces, George abandoned the saw and sauntered off, only to return with a roll of thick black bags. He didn't place much in each one, then carried them over to a door beside the one he'd gone into before, coming to stand in front of her, his face covered in blood now, the freckles gone. The whites of his eyes stood out against all that red.

He stuffed a finger and thumb under the cuff of the white suit and produced what she thought, at first, was a handle of some sort, but with a flick of his wrist, a blade shot out.

"I thought it'd be fitting that you went out the same way as Angie."

He heart hammered so hard, and he walked behind her, grabbing her hair and wrenching her head back. She pissed herself, the fear too great, and the coldness of the knife against her throat brought on that frozen chill from earlier.

Heat, heat on her neck with the slice, the warmth of blood gushing down her chest. She'd go any second now, and it was strange how her brain was still working, how she didn't fight to stay alive anymore but waited for the curtains of death to close on her stage of life. The end came with her vision blackening at the edges, creeping towards the middle, and the last thing she saw was Greg raising a fist in the air, winning his game while she lost hers.

Chapter Thirty

Graham and Victor always took them to houses or parties. It was clear Graham liked Oleksiy, and she played it to her advantage. She shouldn't, it was cruel, but when in a situation like hers, any means of getting away was fair game, and she'd do whatever she had to in order to escape this nightmare.

Sometimes, as she got out of the minibus, he touched her hand—not in a perverted way, more as reassurance. Perhaps he was trying to get across that he understood her predicament, that he wanted to help, but she couldn't let herself believe that. Not yet. Not until she'd spent a couple more months playing out her plan.

Tonight, she and Bohuslava were together — usually, they were kept apart at work. They'd been requested, along with five others, to service a few men at a private gathering in the West End. Graham would be staying with them.

With every new influx of women, some were killed to make room. Others were sold to the highest bidder, the ones who'd tried a little too hard to be what Denny required — it was a fine balance between remaining at the house and being purchased. Oleksiy and Bohuslava lived in constant fear of one of them being selected, then they'd have to part. Denny had said those who'd been bought were kept inside houses all the time, in special rooms, chained up to start with, until Stockholm Syndrome kicked in.

Oleksiy hated it all, how they abused women in this way, how they controlled and manipulated them to the degree that even though what they were being put through was wrong, they agreed to do it anyway. Some sick sense of loyalty to their abuser. She'd never get *that far in. She played the game well, as did Bohuslava, but they refused to form a connection with their Users.*

They were led into a big house. Whoever owned it was rich. She remembered Mother's thoughts on the opulence at Mezhyhirya, how the rich lorded it over the poor without a care. She'd keep that hatred for the ex-president in her mind tonight and transfer it to the homeowner; she wouldn't show it on her face or in her actions, but her thoughts, they'd be filled with how much his status affected them all, how he'd paid for them, yet they wouldn't see a penny of it, Denny and Teo would.

Graham spoke with a man who appeared in a doorway off the foyer. They stared at the women, the man muttering something, then Graham pointed at six of them, the man gesturing for them to follow him. That left Oleksiy. Either she wasn't to the man's taste or someone else wanted her.

"We'll go and sit in the other room and wait, then, I suppose," he said and motioned to a door, likely thinking she hadn't understood a word he'd said.

She followed him into a lounge, and he shut the door. She wondered if he'd come on to her, if he'd take a freebie or was even allowed to do so. He sat on a sofa, his back to the door, and jerked a thumb at the one opposite. She sat, and if Bohuslava had been here, she would have punched Graham and run, but her sister was enduring God knew what, and Oleksiy would never leave her behind.

"This is all bloody disgusting to be honest," he said.

Did he mean the richness of the furnishings or what she was forced to do for a living?

"I'd tell the police, but that Denny… Nah, he'd come after me, not to mention the big boss would have me killed. Did you know we're not meant to tell anyone our names? We're called 'Minion' with a number on the end, but quite frankly, none of us wants to be referred to as that, so Denny said it was all right to use our real names so long as we didn't slip up in front of the boss. He's not around much anyway, Teo, so that's a bonus."

He leant back and closed his eyes. Trusting fellow. She could get up now and stab the poker that stuck out from the fire into his eye, listen to the sizzle as the hot metal burnt everything it touched. She could stab him in the heart with it. Go upstairs and stab that man, too. Free all the women. It looked good in her head but wouldn't work in real life.

Graham opened his eyes. "Listen, if you want me to help you get away, just say the word. I don't even know why I'm mentioning it, you don't know what the fuck I'm saying. But if I can let a couple of you go, at *least I'd have* **done** *something, you know? I could say you'd slipped away when I wasn't looking. Yeah, I'd get a bollocking, but if it was an accident, I reckon Denny would believe it. I mean, look at how what's-her-name almost got out via the back door in the kitchen last week, and he was there, right by her. I'd remind him of that, wouldn't I. I'd say, 'Denny, you know how it goes, how easy it is, so don't come down on me about it.' He'd probably say it was all right for him because he's the boss of the house, but I'd have made my point."*

She stared at him blankly, letting him think she was none the wiser as to what he'd said.

"People would wonder why I'd done it, why I'd taken the risk, but I've known you for ages now, and there's something about you. Do you believe in fate an' all that? My old mum, she used to say there was someone out there for everyone, or several someones — you know, in case one of your soul mates dies or whatever — and if you're destined to be together, you will be. Like it's all mapped out before you're born or some shit. So you were born over there, I was born here, and somehow, we had to meet. It took a war and you lot being basically kidnapped for it to happen, but... Nah, ignore me. It's a bit daft, that."

She'd heard similar from her own mother, how Father had been born in Poland, although his parents had been Ukrainian, and he'd spent most of his childhood miles and miles away. His mother's death meant his father had a hankering to go home, so they'd moved to Ukraine. If they hadn't, maybe Oleksiy's mother would have travelled to Poland at some point, a holiday, and fate would have pushed them together regardless. As it was, they'd met at a dance in Kyiv, and Mother had said it was love at first sight.

Graham looked at Oleksiy that way now, but the feelings weren't reciprocated. She didn't care about him, didn't even find him attractive, but as much as she detested being used, she'd do the same to him if it meant saving her sister.

"It is not this 'daft' you say," she said. "I feel it, too."

He bolted forward, perched on the edge of his seat. "You speak English?"

"Enough. I understand it. I do not speak it well. I hear everything you said."

"Shit. Shit. I didn't think..."

"I will tell no one—if you help me and my sister."

He got up and came over to her, sitting close and holding one of her hands in both of his. "I will, I swear."

She kissed him—she didn't want to but had to. And she let him do what every other man had done since she'd come to England. She transported herself, once again, back to the garden, Father pretending to be upset at them having fun in Kyiv without him, Mother laughing, settling Bohuslava's nerves with promises of syriniki.

Graham finished quickly, clearly nervous about them being caught, and she silently thanked Denny for providing the birth control pill—Graham hadn't used a condom. If she was called to go upstairs, the man would know she'd been used already, Denny might find out, and Graham would be in trouble, so she adjusted her dress, sat, and prayed that wouldn't happen.

Chapter Thirty-One

Teo de Luca sat at Heathrow airport, the picture of calm, when inside he verged on cracking. Unusual for him. A first. Mr Johnson from the party house had refrained from telling him immediately that the police had visited last night, instead informing him at ten o'clock this morning after he'd rolled out of bed with a hangover.

Fuck his hangover.

Teo had phoned Denny, wanting to know if the police had heard about The Network via those two women who'd absconded, but the man's phone had gone straight to voicemail. Typical, Denny was probably ignoring him, worried about getting into trouble.

Teo had sent Minion-66 past the refugee house to check for Denny's sports car or the SUV Patrick used, but neither vehicle had been there. What *was* there were crawling police officers, some of them in white suits, which could only mean they'd been tipped off about the murders. Minion-66 had been stopped, asked where he was going and if he'd seen anything odd in the area recently, and the reply had been no, he was just about to go and see his gran, the excuse 66 always gave. They'd let him go on his way, and Teo had instructed him to get rid of the car he'd used, which was stolen and had no tax or insurance.

Teo had accessed the news, the top story that a body had been found in Daffodil Woods, that of a woman, possibly of European descent. There was no 'possibly' about it, it was one of the refugees, and he'd cursed Denny for being so incompetent in digging a shallow grave—and himself for not being more careful about who he employed.

There were a few possible scenarios.

1. The women had managed to get to a police station and they'd talked.

2. Denny had been arrested, and he'd also talked.

3. Neither of those three had said anything, they'd gone to ground, and someone else had opened their mouths.

Was it the new makeup artist? Denny had assured him she was to be trusted, but wasn't it a little odd that this had blown up after she'd been employed? Had she seen what was going on, heard all about the parties? Had the location of last night's venue been discussed in front of her, and she'd informed the police? Had she witnessed a murder and, horrified, she'd waited for the women to be taken to Johnson's, then she'd made her move?

The ramifications of this were far-reaching, and if Teo wasn't the big boss, he'd be in trouble. As it was, *he* ran The Network, and he answered to no one, although he wished he hadn't gone to London on a whim yesterday. He'd travelled by his real name, but how would he be linked to this mess when to the outsider, he was a mere antiques dealer? Had Johnson already given his name? Had Denny? Were the police on their way here? Or already waiting at the boarding gate to arrest him?

Nerves hatched, ants scurrying through his veins, and he balked at feeling so out of control, at being so smug at the party, thinking the women were too scared to reveal the truth. He was usually so poised, on the ball, yet because of other people's stupid actions, here he was, frightened. *Frightened*, for God's sake, something he'd rarely ever been. If those women hadn't run, none of this would be happening. If Denny had more control over his employees, they would never have been left alone in that toilet by an exit door with a *key* in it.

The more he thought about it, the more he suspected they'd been helped. He knew for a fact Denny wouldn't have aided and abetted them. He knew where he was better off. No, it had to be that man who'd escorted them to the toilet— Graham, wasn't it? Teo couldn't recall his Minion name at the minute. How could he have anticipated the other fellow, Vincent, phoning him for help in the ballroom? Unless they'd cooked it up between them.

Whatever had happened, those men needed to be found, and now Teo had a clear direction in which to go, the fear faded.

He sent an encrypted message to Minion-66.

T: FIND GRAHAM AND VINCENT. END THEM.

MINION-66: DO YOU KNOW WHERE THEY LIVE?

T: YOU KNOW WE DON'T KEEP ADDRESSES. THAT WAY, NO ONE CAN INFORM ON ANYONE.

For the first time, he thought his own rule was stupid. What he wouldn't give to have their place of residence in his little notebook now.

MINION-66: THEY MIGHT BE DOWN THE PUB. I'LL CHECK.

T: YOU DO THAT. BE CAREFUL WHERE YOU DISPOSE OF THEM. THERE WILL BE UNTOLD AMOUNTS OF POLICE AROUND.

MINION-66: THE RIVER?

T: USE YOUR INITIATIVE!

Teo deleted the messages and switched the burner off. He wasn't silly enough to use his contract one when dealing with these people. Anyone who did such a thing deserved all they got. He had everyone's Minion name and numbers in a book in his safe in Italy, so he wiped the phone over with his jacket, even though he had gloves on, then got up and went outside as if for some fresh air. He glanced around for cameras and, seeing one pointed the other way, dropped the burner in a nearby bin. Whatever happened while he was in the air could wait. At home, he'd fire up a new burner, add all the names and numbers, and send out a blanket message, using the code words he always did when he switched mobiles.

He could only pray no one replied with more bad news.

Returning to his seat, he didn't have time to get comfortable. His flight was called, so he made his way to the appropriate gate, visions of his suitcase being taken off the plane and searched through, right now, this second. There wasn't anything incriminating in it, but his laptop... That was in the soft-case bag that hung on his shoulder. If the police awaited him, they'd take it, look through it.

Mio Dio...

But God wouldn't help him now.

Several minutes later, he sat in his first-class seat and dared to stretch his legs out, dared to relax. Twenty minutes after that, he was in the air.

The only hurdles to get over now were the airport at the other end and arriving at his home. If no police were there, he'd consider himself fortunate, then collect one of his fake passports and go to Antigua, remaining there until the dust had settled.

He cared about saving no one's backside but his own.

As Papà had said it should be.

Chapter Thirty-Two

Minion-66 entered The Wheatsheaf and glanced around. Graham and Vincent, Minion-99 and 100 respectively, stood at the bar, pints in hand, heads bent in deep conversation. Conversation it was clear they didn't want anyone overhearing. They didn't know Minion-66 was employed by The Network, he was a 'floater', someone who was available to flit from one job to another for the boss. He knew their real names because they were locals, and he'd been shown their photos, as he always was before people were taken on by The Network, so he could study them for a bit and tell Teo whether they were the type of men to be employed in such a high-risk, top-secret job. He'd given them the go-ahead, telling Teo they didn't seem the kind to grass, they could keep shit to themselves, and as they'd only be drivers, ferrying the women, and bodyguards of sorts while they were dishing out sex, it wasn't as if they'd have access to pertinent information.

Seeing them now, though, he realised he'd probably made a mistake. They had the look of shifty bastards about them, whispering, seeming on edge, and so they should be. With those two women on the loose, the whole outfit could be brought down.

Minion-66 would find out what they'd been up to before he dealt with them.

He strolled over, and Graham elbowed Vincent—to keep quiet? Interesting.

"Minion-66," he whispered so they were aware he was in the know and could be trusted. "Been asked to have a chat about what went on last night. The boss is gunning for Minion-79." Denny.

"Christ, what's wrong with you? We can't talk about it in here." Graham's gaze darted about, as if he thought Teo was lurking somewhere, watching, ready to take him out.

"We'll chat in my van, then."

Minion-66 led the way, his mind going over how he'd play this. He had a stolen Transit, no decals on the sides; he needed it to blend in with all the others. He'd already put fake plates on and loaded up what he'd need before coming here.

Outside, he opened one of the back doors and gestured for them to get in.

"Are you fucking having a laugh?" Graham said. "What's wrong with the front seat?"

Minion-66 sighed. "Nothing, just bloody get in, will you?"

He climbed in and waited by the door until they'd done the same. Graham and Vincent plonked themselves on the bench seat down one side, and Minion-66 shut the door, sitting opposite. He had his gun up one sleeve; that would come out later. For now, he wanted to hear what they had to say.

"The boss is worried one of you two let those women go on purpose," he said.

"What?" Vincent gaped at Graham, then looked at Minion-66. "Why the hell would he think that? Bloody hell, we've been working for him for ages. Why would we suddenly do something stupid now when we know the consequences?"

Minion-66 shrugged. "Just telling you what he said. I told him I'd have a word, get to the truth of it, then we can put it to bed."

"I was gonna say…" Vincent rubbed his forehead. "I don't want any trouble. I've got a wife and kids to feed, know what I mean? I'm not about to put my wages at risk to let some slags run off, not to mention I value my life."

He'd sounded convincing, but Minion-66 knew fear when he saw it, and Vincent was full of it. "That's what I thought. *None* of us want any hassle, do we. So what the hell happened, then?"

Graham nudged his buddy. If it was supposed to be surreptitious, he'd failed. "One of them, don't know her name, she told me she needed the loo. Her and the other one. Fine by me, I thought, and took them to the staff bogs. They went in together—bit weird, but whatever—and then Vinny got hold of me."

Vincent took the baton. "Yeah, there were these two blokes, and they had that look about them, like they were trouble. I assume these people are vetted before they can go to a party, but I dunno, they had that toffee-nosed air, entitled. I rang Graham and told him I needed help in case shit kicked off. Graham came back, and it was just as well, because the toffs jumped on the stage once the curtains went back and tried to paw the women."

"Blimey," Minion-66 said. "Talk about good instincts. So what did *you* do, Graham, before you went back?"

"I told the slags to hurry up and go back to the stage, and if they thought of running, they'd be dead, put in the woods." He laughed, a tad unsteadily. "Denny—urr, Minion-79—always threatens them with that, see. It scares them shitless, and I thought it'd work. Turns out I was wrong, and I've been crapping it ever since in case I got the blame. I mean, what if they tell the police or whatever?"

"That's what the boss is worried about."

"Where are the women, does anyone know?" Graham appeared genuinely worried about them.

Shame he wasn't worried when he let them go. "You're better off telling him all this yourself. He's told me to take you to the hotel he's staying in."

"Shit." Graham shook his head. "Nah, I'm not going anywhere. If he wants to see me, he can come to the pub. People around, you know, so he can't do anything to me."

"Why would he do anything?" Vincent asked. "We haven't done anything wrong."

Well played, but unfortunately, you're lying.

Minion-66 stood, went to the back doors, and pulled his gun out. Pointed it at them. "You need to do as you're told."

"Oh, fuck me, hold up!" Graham raised his hands.

Minion-66 pointed to a bucket with his free hand. "Get two rags out and put them in your mouths."

"W-what?" Vincent's gaze darted to the door.

Minion-66 sighed. "Don't even think about it. I'm happy enough to shoot you in here, I don't care if anyone hears the shots and knows it's me. I can disappear, the boss has got my back."

Graham lowered his hands and took the rags out. He held one out to Vincent and stuffed the other in his mouth.

"Now take a couple of cable ties out and put Vincent's hands behind his back. Secure his wrists and ankles. I'll sort yours afterwards."

"Aww, come on," Vincent said. "There's no need for this, is there? We haven't done anything."

"Then you won't mind seeing the boss, will you. I'm telling you, if you don't do as you're told, I *will* shoot you." Minion-66 waved the gun. "*Do it.*"

Even with a silencer, the gunshots were loud enough to send birds scattering into the air from their perches in the trees. Off they went, soaring on the current while Graham and Vincent soared to the afterlife.

Minion-66 kicked the bodies into the river. He got into the van, not caring if anyone mentioned he'd left The Wheatsheaf with those two. No one knew who he was. He was nothing but a fella with an easily forgettable face.

He smiled and drove off, parking on the outskirts of the East End and torching the vehicle, the gun and his overalls inside. From there, he walked casually for a while, entering The Three Bells then leaving via the back, disappearing into the warren of streets.

He didn't go home. Instead, he opened the door to a flat. Other floater minions came here when they'd done something fishy, needing a bolthole. Unless Teo needed him to do something else, he'd stay here for a week, then go back out into the world.

Murder for The Network really was that simple.

Chapter Thirty-Three

Oleksiy and Bohuslava had just finished giving their longer statements. It had taken four hours. Janine looked as tired as Oleksiy felt. It had been an emotional journey, and she was so relieved the other women had been rescued.

"Our mother," she said. "Did someone contact her?"

"Let me just check that." Janine left the room.

"What if she's dead?" Bohuslava picked at a hangnail. "What if she got bombed and no one can find her in the rubble? What if she's in pieces and they don't know who she is?"

Oleksiy shivered. "Don't think things like that."

They sat in silence.

Janine returned, smiling. "It seems your mum went to stay with your aunt?"

"Lyubov?"

"That's the one." Janine bent and gathered her papers.

"Oh, thank God." Bohuslava leant against Oleksiy.

"Is she okay?" Oleksiy asked.

Janine nodded. "She's fine. She's safer with your aunt, yes?"

"It is in mountains. Would have taken her long time to get there."

"Well, you can stop worrying now, because she's been told you're both fine and have chosen to remain in the UK. She declined to join you."

"She will not leave homeland. We know this."

"Okay, are you ready to go, then?"

They were being taken back to the hotel and would stay there until a proper home could be found. Outside in the car park, while they waited for an officer to drive them there, Janine gestured for them to come closer.

"The taxi drivers. They're sorting a flat for you, and jobs."

Oleksiy raised her eyebrows. "They said they would, but I did not believe."

"They'll help you. Trust them. They're busy at the moment but will be in contact. You've got the phones I gave you, yes?"

Oleksiy patted the carrier bag that contained some more clothes Janine had managed to buy them, despite being busy with The Network case. She was a kind woman. A good woman.

"Your new documents will be ready soon," Janine said.

She felt it was better that they begin afresh, just in case everyone in The Network wasn't apprehended. Two boxes of dark hair dye were also in the bag.

"Thank you," Oleksiy said, tears in her eyes. "We cannot thank you enough."

"No need." Janine smiled. "Ah, the car's here. The officer will stay with you again, although a different one will come later when the shift changes, okay?"

Oleksiy took her sister's hand and led her to the car. They got in the back, and as the vehicle pulled away, Oleksiy waved to Janine, so grateful to her, so grateful for their new lives, given to them by the big taxi drivers.

"Will we see our mother again?" Bohuslava whispered.

"I don't know. I don't know." But Oleksiy hoped they would.

The war would end, wouldn't it?

One day.

Janine returned to the station, going straight to her office. She hadn't had the luxury of sleep. Cadaver dogs had been brought in, and three more bodies had been found in Daffodil Woods, two in another a mile away, all of them chopped up to some degree. Why had the first one been intact? Hadn't the killer had time to use an axe?

There had to be more, and she dreaded hearing that there were. It would be a massive undertaking, working out their identities, informing their relatives, but at least she wouldn't be the one doing that. Selfish to think that, but as with any job, there were aspects she didn't like, and that sort of thing was at the top of the list.

Radburn had gone home at five a.m., too tired to continue, and she'd been relieved. It meant she could nip out and buy things for the sisters without him sticking his oar in, then interview them.

Oleksiy had mentioned something interesting. Graham and Vincent, whoever they were, had helped them to escape. Janine would like to thank them personally for doing the right thing—and ask why they'd accepted jobs in such a horrible organisation if they didn't agree with what was going on. Maybe it hadn't been apparent to begin with. Maybe, because Oleksiy had been having sex with Graham in order to get him to help them—no judgement; in her position, Janine would probably do the same—Graham discovering what the parties were in aid of had pushed him into having second thoughts. Pushed him into planning the escape.

With Keith still overseeing the refugee house and everything being in hand in the woods, Janine really ought to go home, get some sleep. The DCI had spotted her this morning at the front desk and ordered her home then, but she'd explained about the rapport with the sisters, and he understood why she felt she had to stay. She'd promised to leave after the interview, and she gathered her handbag, ready to do just that.

The phone on her desk rang, and she glanced through the glass partition at her team working away, wishing she could ignore the phone and let them deal with it. Wishing she'd left a minute or so earlier, then she wouldn't have heard it.

She sighed and picked up the handset. "Janine Sheldon."

"I don't want you to deal with this, uniforms are there, as is the pathologist, and you're *supposed* to be going home…" The DCI cleared his throat. "But just so you can sleep easier—or maybe it'll make it worse, I don't know—the bodies of a Graham Pritchard and Vincent Wilson have been found in the river by a dog walker. Shot execution style, gagged and cable tied. They floated to the edge and lodged in some reeds before they had a chance to sink."

"Bloody hell…"

"Is that a 'Bloody hell, now I won' t be able to question them'? Or is it like my initial reaction, 'Bloody hell, The Network had them offed'?"

"The last one," she said.

"Hmm. Nasty bunch."

"Have you had a chance to review Oleksiy's and Bohuslava's statements yet?" she asked.

"Err, no."

"Granted, I've not long finished speaking to them, but I thought someone would have passed on the information to you. I did flag it as priority and asked DC Mallard to let you know. Maybe he was too busy…"

"Ah, Mallard was sent out to investigate something so probably forgot. What information are you talking about?"

"Someone called Patrick is in the mix regarding The Network, London accent, black hair and big beard, but the big boss is called Teo de Luca, an Italian."

"Shit, I could have done with knowing about this sooner. Why on earth didn't they tell you those names last night? Ignore me, they were probably traumatised. Okay, I'll get the ball rolling in finding them."

"De Luca's probably flown out of the country by now, seeing as the bodies have hit the news."

"Can't be helped. We'll nab him in the end. Right, piss off. Go home. I don't want to see you until tomorrow morning."

He cut the call, and she stared at the phone, then placed it in the dock. While Graham and Vincent had accepted jobs that contributed to the women's suffering, they *had* done a good deed in the end. Someone out there had ordered for them to be killed, and she hoped they were brought to justice. Unfortunately, she had a feeling that wouldn't come to pass. People who ran these organisations were too clever for words.

For now, all they could do was keep watch at all the ports and airports.

She drove home, wired, still too awake to settle properly in bed yet, so she messaged the twins to let them know the state of play.

GG: ON OUR END, DENNY'S SORTED.

JANINE: I THOUGHT HE WOULD BE. DID HE SAY ANYTHING ABOUT MEN CALLED PATRICK AND TEO?

GG: NOT TEO, BUT WE DID DISCUSS A PATRICK. LANDLORD OF THE BASSETT HOUND.

JANINE: WHAT DOES HE LOOK LIKE?

GG: BLOND, AVERAGE.

She paused.

JANINE: WOULD THE LANDLORD HAVE GONE TO ALL THE TROUBLE OF PUTTING ON A WIG AND FAKE BEARD? WOULD HE HAVE HAD *TIME* TO SPEND AT THE REFUGEE HOUSE? OR IS THE NAME JUST A COINCIDENCE?

GG: FAIR POINT.

JANINE: WHO TOLD YOU ABOUT DENNY AND THE NETWORK?

GG: PATRICK.

JANINE: ARE YOU SURE HE HASN'T GOT ANYTHING TO DO WITH THIS?

GG: I DOUBT IT. HE'S ANGIE'S BROTHER-IN-LAW, SO CAN YOU SEE HIM LETTING DENNY KILL HER IN THE ROBBERY?

JANINE: KEEP AN EYE ON HIM, JUST IN CASE. THE TWO OTHERS WHO HAVE BEEN KILLED, A GRAHAM AND VINCENT. WAS THAT YOU?

GG: NO.

She thought about her recent change of heart regarding Keith, the other DI on the case. She didn't know what she'd been thinking, being prepared to use him on business concerning The Brothers. If they ever found out, she'd be right in the shit. And letting him walk free—what the fuck? Since she'd spoken to Oleksiy and

Bohuslava again today, *no one* should get away with having sex against women's wills.

JANINE: I'VE GOT A JOB FOR YOU. HANG ON, WHICH ONE AM I SPEAKING TO?

GG: GEORGE.

JANINE: GOOD. THERE'S A COPPER WHO NEEDS SORTING. KEITH SYKES, A DI. HE'S SOMETHING TO DO WITH THE NETWORK, EITHER WORKING FOR THEM OR USING THE WOMEN FOR SEX. CURRENTLY AT THE REFUGEE HOUSE OVERSEEING SOCO BUT SHOULD BE GOING HOME SOON AS HE'S PULLED A DOUBLE SHIFT.

She tapped in the address and Keith's phone number.

GG: LEAVE IT WITH ME.

JANINE: YOU SHOULD CONSIDER WHETHER YOUR MOLE DESERVES TO LIVE. HE'S A PART OF THIS. IF HE'S HAD SEX WITH ANY OF THEM...

GG: I'LL TAKE WHAT YOU'VE SAID INTO CONSIDERATION. WE'LL BE MEETING HIM SOON TO DISCUSS HIS FUTURE POSITION WITH US. WE ALSO OWE HIM SOME MONEY FOR HELPING US OUT.

JANINE: IF HE'S INNOCENT IN THAT HE'S JUST A BABYSITTER, FINE, BUT IF HE'S NOT...

GG: HOW ABOUT YOU MIND YOUR OWN BUSINESS THERE.

JANINE: FUCK OFF. I'M GOING TO SLEEP.

GG: SO EARLY?

JANINE: *SOME* OF US DIDN'T GO TO BED LAST NIGHT. LET ME KNOW WHEN KEITH'S DEAD.

She deleted the messages, put all of her phones on charge, *and* on silent, and went for a shower. She'd have beans on toast, couldn't stomach anything else, then try to get some kip.

As the water cascaded over her, she smiled. Before he'd left her this morning, Radburn had said he'd be talking to the DCI about the NCA.

At last, she'd get rid of the pest and prayed whoever took his place wasn't a Nosy Norman. If she had to put up with another one of those, she'd lose her shit.

Chapter Thirty-Four

Honda lived in a narrow two-up, two-down wedged between others of the same ilk. The street appeared higgledy-piggledy, too many houses crammed into one place, too many cars hugging the kerbs, all the wheelie bins on the pavements creating clutter.

George and Greg sat in the work van, forensic suits on, beards and fake glasses, scoping out the vicinity for anyone who was likely to come out and poke their noses in. All was quiet, the late-afternoon sun in a pale-blue sky, people probably making dinner, too busy to look through their windows. It was a chance they were prepared to take, though, being seen. Anyone who butted in would be told, not so politely, to fuck off and take it up with The Brothers.

Honda had arrived home ten minutes ago, his face obscured by a helmet. It hadn't been hard for the twins' men on the streets to discover who he was—with a nickname like that, he couldn't be forgotten, could he. A few shots of brandy brought for someone in the local pub, tongue loosened, said someone had revealed the address, although Denny had been obliging there, too.

"You ready?" George asked.

"Yeah, but once he's sorted, we're going home. I'm knackered."

"You've done nothing but play Xbox, you cheeky bastard."

"Yeah, well, you get tired playing games."

"Do you? I wouldn't know. Too busy killing people and chopping them up."

They left the van, approaching the green front door with a silver gargoyle knocker. It was an ugly little bastard, squashed nose, fat lips, and George raised the loop then let it drop. It clattered twice.

"Who even thinks having something like that is tasteful?" he said.

"Shh, he's coming."

The door opened, and Honda stood there. George knew it was him, even without the helmet, as he had the same jeans on, although he'd taken the leather jacket off. Long hair, stringy, a bit of a fat face which was at odds with his toned body.

"Who the fuck are you?" he said.

George pushed him in the chest and sent him staggering backwards. He entered the house, Greg behind him.

"Oi, who do you think you are? You can't just come in like that!"

"We just did. Shut up whining." Greg closed the door.

Honda stood tall, his chest puffed out, pointer finger waggling. "Get out of my house."

George smiled. "Oh, we will do, once you've got your boots on. We can take you without them, if you like, but for the sake of any neighbours copping an eyeful of your mangy feet… We wouldn't want to upset them unduly, would we."

"I'm not going anywhere."

"Listen to me, you utter dick. You *are* coming with us, and you *will* do as you're told. I'm sick of the likes of you, I've had a bellyful of arseholes already today—who are now dead—so if you wouldn't mind…"

"Of course I fucking mind." Honda seemed to have caught on to George's words because: "Dead? What are you on about? Who?"

"Macey Moorhouse for one, and Denny Rawlings is the other. Then there's a Graham and Vincent, although I won't claim we killed them. That would be lying. Now then, are you going to come quietly, or do I have to knock you out and carry you to the van?"

"Bloody hell, what did you kill *them* for?"

George sighed and said to Greg, "Why do people always feel the need to know the ins and outs of the cat's arsehole?"

"Dunno, bruv."

George stared at Honda. "They're dead because they stole from us, as did you, and as for

Graham and Vincent, I suspect The Network got hold of them."

"I don't even know who you are, so how can I have stolen from you?"

"Vintage Finds?"

Honda paled. "Ah fuck."

"Ah fuck, indeed. Are you aware that's our shop? We're George and Greg Wilkes, by the way."

Honda shook all over. "What? I know jack shit about you owning that shop. Denny didn't say anything about that. All he told me was that there were goods in the counter we had to nick and that the woman behind the till would be easy to— And anyway, The Brothers don't have beards, so unless they've grown overnight, you're not them."

George peeled his beard back a bit at one sideburn, thinking of what Janine had said about that Patrick bloke. Did he use a fake beard, too?

Nah, he hasn't got it in him to be involved.

Honda reared his head back. "Fucking Nora."

George barked, "Leave Nora out of it. Angie. You killed her. Why?"

"Denny told me to, didn't he."

"Would you jump off a cliff he told you to an' all?"

"No!"

"Sounds to me like you'll do anything he says. Said—he can't order anyone about anymore. Are you getting your boots on or what?"

Honda spun and darted down the hallway into a room. George inhaled a deep breath—he'd suspected this would happen—and took off after him, naffed the hairy bastard wanted to play silly buggers. He took his gun out of his cuff just in case Honda had grabbed a weapon, then walked into the room. The pleb tried to open the patio doors in the lounge, all fingers and thumbs, glancing over his shoulder from time to time in panic.

"I'd stop trying if I were you," George said. "I'd rather you came with us so I can kill you elsewhere, but if I *really* have to, I'll do it here." He held the gun up.

Honda turned, his hands raised. "All right, okay. Fuck."

George grinned. "Good boy. You know it makes sense."

In the warehouse, the third body of the day cut up and deposited in the Thames, Greg actually helping this time, George had a shower and put a clean grey suit on. He'd shot Honda in the head, couldn't be arsed to torture the gimp, and he'd contacted the crew to come and clean up the mess made by Honda, Denny, and Macey.

"You know you said you wanted to go home?" George smiled.

Greg stared at him, pissed off. "Fuck's sake, what now?"

"I want to have a word with Beaker, get his role sorted, ask about Patrick to get a bead on whether he could be the same one from the refugee house."

"Why does it have to be today?"

"I want to check he's on the level. Then I want to nip to that flat we've just had decorated, see if it's up to scratch, because those two poor cows are staying at a hotel and I want them more settled."

"Soft arse. They'll be fine there for a few days."

"I know, but they've been through so much shit. If we can make it better, I'd want to do it sooner rather than later."

At Beaker's flat, white suits, beards, and glasses off, they went up to the balcony and knocked on the door. He opened it—at first, George didn't think it was him, then the realisation dawned that the kid had dyed his hair. Sensible. If he grew a beard and dyed that, he'd be unrecognisable, but in the meantime, George would suggest a fake.

"Fuck me, is everything all right?" Beaker stepped back to allow them to go in.

"We'll soon see."

George stepped in, Greg behind him, and they followed Beaker to the kitchen.

"Want a drink or summat?" Beaker asked.

"Can do. Something cold."

"I've got Coke. *Proper* cans."

"Lovely." George leant against the sink unit.

Greg remained by the door, taking a can off Beaker. "Cheers."

George received his and popped the tab. Had a few sips. Told Beaker everything that had been going on since they'd last seen him. "What I want to know is, did you ever shag any of the women?"

"You what?" Beaker gaped at him. "No I fucking didn't! For one, that would be wrong, and two, Denny would have killed me. If he didn't, someone else would have. I looked after them as best I could, gave them water, let them use the loo. Chris was the same."

"I was just about to ask about him. Where is he?"

"Gone to stay with his aunt in Manchester. Thought it was best he kept out of the way."

"Right. Spoken to your nan, have you?"

"Yeah, she's loving it."

"Good. Patrick…"

"What about him?"

"Know much?"

"He's just some gruff bastard who ferries Denny around, and from what I could make out, he might have killed some women."

"What's he look like?"

"Black hair and beard. Deep voice."

"So nothing like Patrick from the Bassett Hound, then?"

"No way! They couldn't be more opposite."

Satisfied with that, although George would be vigilant when they next visited the pub, he said, "Okay, let's discuss your new job, shall we? I'll preface it by saying that if you ever, *ever* fuck us about, you'll be dead—and we're not talking a Denny threat, we're talking proper, shit-your-pants, killed-in-our-warehouse threat, understand?"

"Yeah, yeah. I get it. I won't fuck you about, I swear."

George believed him and tossed an envelope with five grand inside it on the table. "Make sure you don't."

Make sure you don't. That wasn't like Denny would say it. George's words held so much more sincerity and promise. Beaker reckoned if he so much as dipped the tip of his little toe in other waters, he'd have a Cheshire smile.

They'd gone, the twins, off to check some flat for Oleksiy and Bohuslava. Nice blokes, when you thought about it. Beaker was well lucky they'd believed what he'd told them. It was the truth anyway, but it could have gone the other way. Denny, Macey, and Honda were dead, and the shocker of it all, Graham and Vincent had been *shot*, for fuck's sake, but George and Greg hadn't done it. Had to be The Network, didn't it, and Beaker was glad they didn't know where he lived. Like he'd thought before, he could have been followed, though.

Maybe he should leave his flat after all. The twins had said that was the better option and had left him to think about moving into one of theirs. They bought flats on the regular, they said, did them up, rented them to people who worked for them. Yeah, nice blokes.

The doorbell went, and he chuckled, thinking they'd forgotten to tell him something. He didn't bother with the peephole and flung the door open. "What did you—"

"Minion-66," the man said, gun raised.

Lights out.

Patrick stood outside his house having a cheeky fag before he went to the hospital to collect Liv and her mother. The old dear had come round, and the tests she'd had showed her body had kept her asleep because of the shock of losing Angie. Low blood pressure.

Denny hadn't been answering his phone, nor had he called or messaged, so Patrick had been stuck at the hospital all day with the wife, bored off his tits. He'd nipped home to let the dog out an hour ago, but he'd best be getting back. He didn't fancy having his ear chewed off.

A motorbike pulled up, and at first he thought it was Honda, but the vehicle wasn't a Honda, so no, it couldn't be him. The visor went up, and a pair of eyes peered at him.

"Minion-66."

"Right…"

The rider's arm rose, and Patrick stared at the business end of a gun.

His guts rolled. "Hang on a second…"

"No loose ends. Night-night."

Chapter Thirty-Five

A t half past nine, the evening matching the chill of the morning, his lapel minus a crocus, George sat opposite Janet, thinking he was a bit of an arsehole, making out this was another date. Telling her in public was a coward's game—she'd hold back any hysterical emotions, then, although like he'd said to Greg, he reckoned she'd act like she didn't give a shit anyway, self-preservation. They'd eaten dinner, making small talk, and now sat with coffees. He waited for her to start on at him, like she always did lately at the end of a meal, anger boiling just at anticipating what she'd come out with. It had been difficult to maintain a pleasant air from the moment he'd walked into the restaurant and she'd kissed his beard-covered cheek. Now it was over in his mind, this charade seemed unnecessarily cruel. She'd see it that way, too. Would perhaps have preferred to be let down gently in the comfort of her own home.

He didn't like himself for his decision to do it this way. There was still time to change it, though. Drop her off, tell her in the car. Watch her get out of it, tears in her eyes, rushing up her garden path. Maybe he was being presumptuous, conceited. She might not cry at all. He might not mean as much to her as he'd thought.

Just take her home.

"You've been on edge all evening," she said. "What's going on?"

Here we go.

"We're not working, are we." He looked her in the eye.

"I'm certainly not. I haven't turned therapist on you all night." She smiled.

Makes a change. "I didn't mean that."

"Oh. You mean us."

"Hmm."

She leant back. "No, we're not. I wanted to have a chat with you about it actually... Wasn't sure when the right time was to bring it up. While I was away on that course...well, it gave me a few days to think. I came back, and when I saw you again, my mind went the other way, so I kept my mouth shut. But..."

He hadn't expected that, for her to bin him before he binned her, if that's what was going on here. He'd let her have the lead. Let her think she was the one ending it—unless she suggested ways to fix it, then he'd have to wade in and put a stop to any thoughts that they could even do that nonsense.

"Go on," he said.

"We can't move forward until you acknowledge you have...issues."

She just can't give it up, can she. "I can acknowledge I do, I just don't need them to have a label. To be pushed and pushed to *accept* a label.

To have it rammed down my throat at every opportunity."

She sighed. "I'm not even going there. It's clear what your thoughts are about it. I don't think I'll ever know you, not really. You've opened up a lot since I first met you, so that's good progress, but I don't believe I'll ever know the real you." She paused. "You won't let me."

He recalled a meme he'd seen the other day, one he'd learnt by heart for this moment. It had struck such a chord with him, that if she didn't understand when he repeated it to her, she never would. "You won't see it for what it is, until you stop looking through the lens of what you want it to be."

She widened her eyes. "That's philosophical of you."

"But it's true."

"So you're saying—again—that I'm trying to change you."

"Yep."

"I'm trying to *help*."

"So you keep saying. You want me to be someone I'm not, and I'm not prepared to change for you."

"Then I'm not the right person for you."

"No."

He didn't bother saying she'd been coming across as one of *those* people who liked him for the most part but there were a few things that didn't fit her idea of a cookie-cutter partner and she wanted to fine-tune him—because wasn't he doing the same? *He* didn't like parts of *her*, wished she'd pack it in with attempting to mould him, and it seemed she was just as stubborn as him because she wasn't prepared to stop her quest of having the perfect man for her. Once she'd realised he wasn't allowing it, she was backing off. He couldn't work out if that meant she had narcissistic traits or if she'd plain given up.

"So this is it, then?" While she must have made the decision to end it, tears still glossed her eyes.

He had to admit, his itched with a prickle. They'd been great together at first. "Yeah. I don't have to give you a warning, do I?"

"No. Your secrets are safe with me. I loved you—still do actually—but we're not suited. I'm not about to phone the police, and I certainly won't go round yours, steal your clothes, and burn them in your car."

"Nah, I didn't take you for a bunny boiler." He still maintained eye contact. "Cheers for giving enough of a shit to try and fix me, though. But it was never going to happen. I'm too far gone."

"I don't agree, but it doesn't matter. Will you still need me for therapy?"

"Best not, eh?"

Funny, now it had come to an end, she wasn't getting on his nerves.

"Want a lift home?" he asked.

"I'll phone for a taxi." She rose, came to stand beside him, and flicked his ear instead of her usual goodbye kiss. "Look after yourself."

Then she was gone.

It had been too easy, the parting of ways, and the excess energy he'd been left with had to go somewhere. In the van, in a side street, he finished off his Ruffian disguise and looked at himself in the rearview mirror.

"You'll do."

He got out, climbed in the back, and put his forensic gear on, including a mask. Suitably togged up, he drove to Keith Sykes' street and parked two doors down. He'd roped in Dwayne, their car thief, to sit outside the property and let him know when Sykes arrived home, swearing him to secrecy. Sykes had turned up about six, then a woman and two kids had left. Window open, Dwayne had picked up a conversation as they'd clambered into their car. They were going bowling then having dinner at Frankie and Benny's.

Ruffian glanced at the clock on the dash. Ten o'clock, so he was cutting it fine. The family could be back shortly. He'd better get a shift on.

Out of the van, lock pick in gloved hand, he checked the vicinity for any cameras and Ring doorbells. Nothing as far as he could see, but it didn't matter, he had his disguise, the van had false plates, and Janine would just have to cover up shit, considering he was doing this for her. He hadn't told Greg about the Sykes murder, a new secret, but that was guilt he'd deal with later.

At the front door, he quickly got it open, tucked the pick up his left sleeve, took the gun from his right, and entered. Kept the door ajar for a fast getaway. Dwayne had said Sykes was in the front bedroom—he'd seen him at the window, closing the curtains. As the bloke had done a double shift, he'd be in a deep sleep, and Ruffian could shoot him without the copper knowing he'd been there, a clean, simple kill. But Ruffian didn't like simple, he liked danger, thrills, so he climbed the stairs knowing he was going to wake the bastard up.

He found the correct bedroom, conscious of the time frame, and went inside, standing next to someone whose features he couldn't see in the murk. He reached for the lamp and switched it on. Ah, there he was. Eyes closed—*I want to see what colour they are*—mouth open, the tips if his top teeth peeking out. Skin scored with lines of tiredness; mouth brackets, crow's feet. A pasty pallor, porridge-coloured. His eyebrows needed trimming, as did his nose hair. It was that long, one of them curled out around his nostril. His brown barnet needed a serious cut.

The funeral parlour will sort him out.

Ruffian turned, parted the curtains an inch, checking the street. The family car, a red SUV, wasn't out there. He gave Sykes his attention again, shoving his shoulder.

"Oi, wake up."

A snort, segueing into a long snore.

"I *said*, wake *up*!" Ruffian pressed on the bloke's chest.

Sykes' eyes opened slowly, unfocused, and he stared at Ruffian, maybe thinking he was in a dream, his sleep-drugged brain taking a while to catch up. Then his police instinct kicked in, and he went to bolt upright, but Ruffian held him down and placed the end of the gun at his temple, the silencer long, an accomplice in getting the job done quietly.

Blue eyes, full of fear.

"Janine says goodbye."

A second of realisation for Sykes, then Ruffian pulled the trigger.

A car engine, the rumble getting closer. He peered out through the gap in the curtains again, adrenaline pumping at the sight of headlights sweeping into the little driveway. Ruffian left the lamp on, left the room, closing the door, and rushed downstairs. He planted his back to the hallway wall—someone approached the front door—then darted into the toilet, locking himself in. If anyone tried to enter, they'd think Sykes was in there, and it would buy Ruffian some time.

A key in the lock. The front door must have closed by itself while he'd been upstairs.

Laughter.

"That bit was brilliant," someone said. The daughter?

"So funny. Right, up to bed now." Definitely the mum.

"Can't we stay up a bit longer?" The son.

"No, you know the score. We've got to get up early tomorrow. Unless you don't want to go to Chessington…"

Ah, they thought they were off to a theme park. Shame they wouldn't be going. They'd be too cut up to do anything like that.

The scrape of a door chain being secured. *Fuck.* Footsteps, the obvious tromp upstairs. Different ones, the *tap-tap-tap* of the mother walking down the laminated floor of the hallway? A muted flick, the light, then another—the kettle?

Ruffian crept out. Glanced down at the light coming from the kitchen. He reached out blindly for the chain, made contact, cursing its tinkle. Slowly, with his sights still on the kitchen, he drew the chain across. Had to look at it as he carefully let it go. He took hold of the Yale knob and twisted. Switched his gaze back to the kitchen. His heart lurched. The wife stood at the sink, frozen, staring at his reflection in the window, the darkness outside showing them up in stark clarity. She spun, her hand to her chest, and opened her mouth to scream.

"Don't," he said, raising the gun. "The Network sent me."

"Who...?"

"You'll find out."

"What...what have you done?"

She'll find that out an' all.

He wrenched the door open, stepped out. Walked casually to the van. Calm. Collected. The excitement of it all buzzed through him. Enriched his blood.

Even more so when a scream tore from the house.

He drove away, keeping to the back roads, eventually ending up at the breaker's yard where his man took over the disposal of the vehicle. He collected another car Dwayne had nicked, took his disguise and protectives off, then drove to the Bassett Hound. Inside, he approached Nance who looked like she'd been crying.

"You all right?" he asked.

She shook her head. Came forward to whisper, "Patrick's been shot. Was it you?"

Ah, so he *was* part of The Network. "Nope, but thanks for the info."

He dumped the car a few streets away and continued his journey home on foot as George, forensic suit and disguise rolled up under his arm.

He entered, going straight to the living room, Greg on the sofa watching telly. Everything on the fire, burning nicely, George sat and toyed with the gun.

"Shit." Greg stared at him. "Did you end up having to kill her?"

"Janet? Nah."

"So who *did* you kill?"

"Someone in The Network."

"What?"

"Janine asked me to do it."

"Bloody hell…"

"It was a copper."

"Oh, Jesus Christ, George! They're going to be all over that, pull out all the stops."

"Not when they find out he's bent. They won't give a fuck then."

"How will they even know?"

George smiled. "I told the wife."

"What? How the hell did you let her see you?"

"Her and the kids came home as I was leaving."

Greg puffed air out. "This had better not come back to bite us. You, going out on your own."

"It won't. Patrick's copped it—and before you start, no, it wasn't me."

"So he *was* a part of it, then."

"Yeah, got shot apparently." George leant back. Needed a change of subject. "Janet basically ended it before I had the chance."

"Aww, did she realise she couldn't get her own way in changing you?"

"Probably." George stood. "Fancy a Pot Noodle?"

Chapter Thirty-Six

Teo cursed. Sykes hadn't answered his messages, nor had he picked up when Teo had phoned him. Maybe the copper was busy at work and it wasn't safe for them to talk. But Teo needed information on how the investigation was going, inside information that wouldn't be on the news. Sykes had been a Godsend so far, ensuring anything iffy was swept under the carpet. He'd better continue to do so or…

There was only one thing for it. Teo rang Minion-66. "It's not another kill, don't worry."

Minion-66 laughed. "Wouldn't care if it was. You know me, I'm a ghost."

Teo thought about the body of that lad in the flat, how Minion-66 had left him half in the front doorway, half out, a clear message to any other Minions that they'd get the same if they didn't keep their mouths shut. The five grand he'd found inside? Teo had told him to keep it as a bonus, then ordered him to shoot Patrick. Then there were the other two, 99 and 100, making the news.

TWO MEN, SHOT EXECUTION STYLE, DUMPED IN RIVER!

The rest of the employees would get the idea. No matter that the police crawled all over the refuge house, one of many, they'd know they had to sit tight and do as he'd asked when he'd sent a blanket message earlier on his new burner, opening with telling them it was the boss: IL CAPO, then: NO PARTIES FOR A MONTH. NO PICKUPS AT THE DOCKS. LIE LOW. AWAIT MY NEXT INSTRUCTION.

"What do you need?" Minion-66 asked.

"A check on Twelve."

"Right. I'll let you know what's going on."

Teo pressed the END CALL button and smiled. He could always count on 66 to get the job done right.

In disguise, Minion-66 strode down Sykes' street. Police cars and a large van had parked outside, every window in the house lit, a cordon blocking off a section of the road. He approached the copper standing by the tape three doors down from Sykes' place.

"Shit, can't I get past?"

"Afraid not. Where are you off to at this time of night?"

"Been to the pub. I'm on my way home. Live with my gran."

"Did you walk this way to the pub?"

"Nah, I went down Portland Avenue."

"Right."

"What's happened?"

"Murder inquiry, sir. Do you know a Mr Sykes at all?"

"Nope."

"Okay, on you go."

Minion-66 turned and walked back the way he'd come. Round the corner, he took his burner out and messaged the boss.

MINION-66: 12 IS DEAD, AND IT WASN'T ME.

BOSS: FUCK.

Teo had boarded the plane, destination Antigua. He had a nine-hour journey ahead and tried to settle his nerves with the in-flight offering of alcohol. He was now Paolo Campagna, and he had sufficient funds in a bank account in that name, plus credit cards. His financial man in Italy had ensured the police, should they be aware a Teo de Luca needed apprehending, wouldn't find any properties in that name. No cars registered. Everything belonged to Paolo and another alias, Ugo Franchitti, and had done for years. The trail would go cold for them the second they discovered Teo had landed in Italy earlier. The only worry he had was locals, and the police in his town, knowing Teo de Luca had lived there.

Hopefully, it wouldn't come to his real name being blackened, parroted out of newsreaders' mouths so the townsfolk became aware of who he really was. It would be such a shame to have to go without their adoration, but if necessary, he could start again with his angel disguise and gain the love of the locals in Antigua.

"There is always hope, even when everything around you is in ashes," Papà had once said after one of his trips down memory lane about Mamma.

Paolo wouldn't only be an angel, he'd be a phoenix, rising, rebuilding, becoming great again while The Network continued to draw in revenue, the money laundered then put into Paolo's and Ugo's banks, as it always had been since Papà's death.

He'd learnt from the master.

No one would take him down.

No one.

Chapter Thirty-Seven

George woke up to news on the radio that boiled his piss. A Nigel Lott had been found dead on his doorstep by the man who ran the chippy downstairs. Beaker. George's instinct was to go round there, to wreak havoc, but with the police in attendance, that would be the worst move he could make.

Greg came into the kitchen, suited and booted, all ready to collect Oleksiy and Bohuslava from the hotel. Janine had gone there to relieve the guard officer of his duties so no one thought it odd the women were walking off with two gangsters.

"What's got your goat?" Greg asked.

"Beaker's been offed."

"*What?*"

"You heard me. Poor kid."

"It's The Network."

"Yep. I've let Janine know he's our mole and that Patrick was in with Denny."

"Fuck me sideways." Greg poured a coffee and sat at the island.

George, having been bored waiting for him to appear, had managed to make beans on toast without burning anything. He took Greg's plate over and sat beside him.

"You not having any?" Greg asked.

"I had mine while you took yonks to get ready."

"I needed a shave."

"So did I. *And* I plucked my nose hairs."

Greg stared at him. "Why did I need to know that?"

"Because when I saw the state of Sykes', it got me paranoid."

Greg shook his head and cut into his toast. "Fucking wally."

While his brother ate, George contemplated what Janet was doing, whether she was okay, despite her brave front. Then he imagined Beaker's nan having to cut her holiday short because her grandson had been shot in the fucking forehead. Then there was Liv, not only losing her sister but her husband, too. George could only hope she never found out what he'd been getting up to behind her back.

Would The Network hunt Chris down in Manchester and kill him, too? Jesus, that outfit was merciless, but he had to scrub it all from his head. They'd done what they could, and now they had to move on. It was the police's job now.

"Janine's got her plate full at the minute," he said.

"I bet."

"Her DCI told her he wanted her on his section of the investigation now—finding everyone in The Network, plus finding who killed Sykes."

"That's good. Means she can keep a close eye on what's happening. I didn't sleep much last night, worrying you'd get caught for it."

"Everything's in order."

"If you get nicked and I have to do this shit alone…"

"Eat your breakfast and shut up." George left him to it, going into the living room to check the fire had done a sufficient job in scoffing his kill disguise last night. He got on with cleaning the ashes out, then flushed them down the toilet. Back in the kitchen, he leant on the doorjamb and watched Greg stacking the dishwasher. "Come on, we've got people to make happy."

They left the house in their BMW, George clearing his mind of the unpleasantness and filling it with the idea of doing nothing but good today. It'd save him going mad with anger.

Hair now brown, Oleksiy wandered around the smelling-of-fresh-paint flat, Bohuslava close on her heels. Her sister was wary around their guardian angels, didn't want to be left alone with them, and Oleksiy couldn't blame her. This all seemed too good to be true, but the twins had stuck to their promise. Here was the flat, furnished, everything perfect, and a credit card in the name of Mr G Wilkes was on the side in the kitchen so they could go and buy some new clothes, shoes, whatever they wanted. George had said they'd discuss their jobs tomorrow. Today was for treating themselves.

Janine had handed them new identities, and Oleksiy suspected they weren't genuine, that the twins had something to do with it. It would be weird, thinking of herself as Irina, Bohuslava as Kalyna, but they'd have to get used to it. George had told them, on the way here, that Denny, Graham, Vincent, Patrick, and the kind man who'd brought the water had been killed, so The Network were intent on wiping out anyone who posed a problem.

"If you keep your heads down, noses clean, you'll be all right," he'd said.

In one of the bedrooms, Bohuslava shut the door and leant on it. She must have been waiting for them to be alone. "I don't trust them."

"Not yet, but Janine said they're on our side. Look at everything they've done for us already."

"We were promised things before."

"There's a difference. Those promises were lies, they were broken. These ones are coming true. It'll take time, I know that, but we'll be okay."

"What work is it? What if they make us have sex?"

"Then we'll tell Janine." There was only one way to solve this, to stop Bohuslava from scaring herself to death, so Oleksiy gestured for her to move out of the way then took her hand, guiding her back to the living room. "My sister is worried. About jobs. What we will do. We must know you are telling truth."

George smiled. "Shit, I should have realised you'd need reassurance. We've got this shop. Vintage Finds. We need someone to run it."

"What shop is it?"

"All old stuff. You know, vintage. Old-fashioned. The shop needs, err, cleaning up a bit, but once it's sorted, you can start work." He took his phone out and showed them pictures of the exterior and interior.

Bohuslava gasped—it was her kind of place.

"We will work *there*?" she asked Oleksiy.

"Yes."

"I like this shop." Bohuslava smiled, for the first time in a long while seeming okay, relaxed. "I think we will be happy here now."

Relieved, Oleksiy nodded at the twins. "We will do it."

George's grin lit up her heart, because he *was* a kind man, he *was* good, it shone from him.

He went on to explain they were leaders, how it worked, and as their employees, Oleksiy and Bohuslava would be kept safe.

"If anyone touches you, we'll kill them," he said.

She believed him, but it didn't scare her like Denny had. It filled her bones with courage, and she knew, without a doubt, no one would ever hurt them again.

Chapter Thirty-Eight

Zoe, blindfolded, had left the safe house and now stood in her own kitchen, pleased as punch to be back but wishing it was like the one in the home where she'd so recently stayed. She shouldn't be ungrateful, should be chuffed with what she already had, but still, she'd seen how her place could look to a stranger, and there wasn't any harm in dreaming about a renovation, was there?

Her sons had gone back to school with a warning not to say where they'd been nor who'd sent them there—and especially not to their father. She'd had to come clean about who she worked for, and far from looking at her in a bad light, the kids had told her they reckoned it was bloody brilliant to have George and Greg as a boss and they'd be asking them for jobs when they were older.

She'd shivered at that. What if her boys grew into strapping men who'd be used for violence and murder? She'd worry her arse off if that happened, but she wouldn't stand in their way. Their lives, their choices, although she'd try to steer them away from it, of course. What mother would gladly send their kids out when there was a high possibility they'd get killed?

She stacked the dishwasher and set it on eco, pushed the ON button, and went over to the kettle. She'd cleaned this place all morning, ashamed at how grubby it had seemed when she'd walked back in. Compared to the safe house, it was a grot box. While the water boiled, she viewed things critically, and if she were honest, all it needed was a fresh coat of paint, maybe a few throws and new curtains.

The doorbell went, and she rushed to answer it, thinking it was probably The Brothers. They'd mentioned they had another mission for her and wanted to discuss it. She would normally have met them at Vintage, but now the police had cleared it as a crime scene, the twins' crew were in there, cleaning up the evidence of a murder.

She stared through the peephole. Shit, it was Pete.

She flung the door open. "What do you want? What have I told you about coming here?"

"I need help," he said.

"What have you done now, fucked things up with your girlfriend? Christ, when will you ever learn, eh?"

"No, she doesn't know about the one-night stand."

He'd said it as if *Zoe* already knew, like he'd forgotten he hadn't told her. "Fucking hell. At least there's no kids involved with her." She folded her arms, showing her refusal to let him in.

"Can we talk inside?"

379

"Err, no. I don't want your manky self in my place, thanks, I've just gone through it like a dose of salts."

"Zoe, come on. You've always been my best friend, always know how to sort things when I fuck up."

"Best friends don't piss-arse about behind their wife's backs. And we're no longer together, so thankfully, your cock-ups aren't mine to fix anymore."

He leant forward and whispered, "I've killed someone."

Her stomach flipped. "*What*?"

"Some drug pusher. Well, I thought he was pusher, but it turns out he was a buyer. And so was the woman who's dead an' all."

"What woman? What the fuck are you on about?" She froze, realising who he meant. "Not those two who've been on the news?"

"Yeah."

"Jesus fucking wept. Get in here, and don't touch anything. I don't want your mucky hands on my nice clean surfaces."

He pelted inside, shooting off down the hallway. She shut the door and followed, telling herself she was only hearing him out because he was her son's father. No other reason. She didn't love him anymore, so why else *would* she help him?

She joined him in the kitchen, and he sat at her table, his hands splayed on the wood, his smile at odds with what he'd just told her. How the fuck could he smile at doing *exactly* what she'd asked him not to when he'd confessed to murder?

"Joking, by the way," he said. "I didn't kill anyone. I just needed you to let me in."

Hatred for him rose, as wicked as when she'd discovered he'd cheated on her. "Get out."

"Aww, don't be like that. Make us a cuppa and a bacon sarnie, will you?"

"Don't be like that? You've just shit the life out of me, put me in an awful position, and now you think I'll make you some lunch? Fuck right off."

"You must still love me if you were prepared to help."

"I did it for the *kids*, Pete, not you. When will you bloody grow up?"

The doorbell ding-donged again, and she fought the urge to scream. She left him and his grin, stalking down the hallway, wishing Pete was dead. Yes, she detested him that much, and the only reason he was still breathing was the fact her sons would be upset if he died.

She opened the door, but no one was there. She went out, thinking whoever it was would be in the street, but again, no one. She stepped back indoors, slamming the door shut, and marched to the kitchen. "Fucking knock door ginger. Right, sod off. I mean it. If you don't go, I'm ringing The Brothers."

"Like *you* have their phone number." Pete stood and ambled past her. "I'll pick the boys up on Friday, then."

"You do that—*if* they want to go. They're on about going to the cinema with their mates."

He strutted off, cock of the walk, and she resisted grabbing the boiled kettle, running after him, and pouring the lot over his fucking head. The door clicking shut doused her anger somewhat, so she turned to make her tea. The wall cupboard to the right of the sink unit caught her eye. The door was slightly open, and she *knew* she'd shut it because she'd scrubbed the life out of it earlier. Her heart sank. In there was the tin she kept the Disneyland money in. Stupid to collect it all in cash, but she'd wanted to see it growing, wanted to take her boys to Florida for a trip of a lifetime.

Not wanting to, because it meant she'd find out Pete really *was* a bastard, she opened the cupboard and reached for the tin at the back. It was pretty one, silver, with doves etched into it. She lifted the lid and looked inside.

The money was gone. All seven grand of it.

"You *arsehole*!" she shouted.

There was no point running after him, he'd have driven off by now. One of her boys must have let slip it was there, been excited about going on holiday once she'd finally finished saving. She'd only told them the other night.

She thought of everything Pete had ever done to her, all the pain he'd caused.

Did that deserve death? She reckoned so now, but that was because she was livid. How would she feel when she calmed down?

She picked up her phone and sent the twins a message.

I NEED TO SPEAK TO YOU. URGENTLY.

George and Greg seemed to fill the dining area of her kitchen they were that big. She'd told them what Pete had done, assured them her sons wouldn't have done anything so rotten, and now, everyone was quiet.

Until George piped up. "That deserves a knee-capping and a warning at the very least."

"Okay." She nodded. "What about the money, though? He's probably got himself into debt, gambling, and it'll be long gone."

"We'll double your wages until you've saved it again, all right?" Greg said.

Tears filled her eyes. "You two are so fucking *nice*."

George snorted. "There are a fair few who'd beg to differ. Are you going to tell your lads what he's done?"

"Do you think I should?"

"Look, it sounds to me like you've shielded them enough from him. It's about time they realised what a bastard he really is. They're old enough to take it." George shrugged.

"Okay, don't tell me when you're knee-capping him else I'll be a bundle of nerves. I'd rather find out afterwards." She straightened her spine. "Right, let's talk about better things. What's my next job?"

"We want you to spend the majority of your time out the back at Vintage. Keep an eye on Oleksiy and Bohuslava, although they've got new names now. Irina and Kalyna."

She chuffed out a laugh. "What good am I going to be in protecting them?"

"It's not protecting. We want to make sure they've completely broken away from The Network—or that they weren't followed that night and someone knows where they are. Keep an eye out, see if anyone comes in and talks to them in their language, that sort of thing. Follow them if they leave the shop."

"That's easy enough. What's my excuse for being there?"

"A translator if they need one, someone to answer questions about stuff until they settle in. I'm sure they're kosher, but we just want to be sure."

Zoe nodded, so gutted about the money but grateful she could save it again quickly.

The twins really were angels.

George left Zoe's, his ire so great he had murder on his mind. Ruffian whispered to him about killing Pete, to get rid of him permanently so Zoe didn't have him in her life anymore. Was it his right to do that when she hadn't agreed to it, though? There were her sons' feelings to take into consideration, too.

In the van, Greg said, "Don't even think about it."

"What!" George grinned. "Stop reading my mind."

Greg pinched his bottom lip. "Although saying that, he did upset one of our employees..."

"Hmm."

"And we could wait until a few months have passed so she doesn't twig it's us. Stage it so it looks like a random attack. A fatal one. Warn Janine to cover our tracks."

George ruffled Greg's hair. "You're the best brother."

Greg put his seat belt on. "Well, why don't you try being the best brother an' all and drive to the Taj, I'm starving, and if we see that scrote on our travels, we'll just happen to knock him over then drive away."

George roared with laughter, Ruffian appeased.

For now.

Chapter Thirty-Nine

Genevieve had already had enough of Pete. She didn't know how his ex had put up with him for all of those years. What had Genevieve ever seen in him? Why had she fancied him? Maybe it was him being an older man that had done it. She was younger than him, granted, possibly swayed by his attention in the boozer of an evening, but come on!

She suspected he'd been having an affair or had at least shagged someone after a bender at the pub. The not knowing had been driving her as mad as him picking the hard skin off his feet and leaving it on the kitchen floor. *And* he didn't wash his hands afterwards. She couldn't talk, she had a secret of her own, but still…

He was a total munter, and she wished she'd never met him, but he lived in her flat now, had made himself right at home, and she wasn't sure she could get him to move out without him causing a fuss.

Could she approach The Brothers about a situation like this? No, she doubted they got involved in domestics.

The thing was, she worked for Debbie during the day, although Pete didn't know that. He thought she was one of those call centre people who dealt with insurance claims, not a tart who stood on the corner and prayed he never decided to have a bevvy in The Angel and saw her standing there, touting for business.

She didn't need him for his money, she earnt enough on her own, thanks, but she *had* wanted him for stability, someone to come home to at the end of the day. Maybe she should tell him what she really did. That'd shock him, disgust him, and he'd leave, wanting nothing to do with her anymore.

He'd come home three months ago, boasting he'd nicked seven grand off Zoe, a holiday fund, and she'd watched him steadily fritter it away on beer, gambling, and new clothes. She hadn't wanted anything to do with it, had warned him if The Brothers found out they'd be gunning for him, but too much time had passed now, so Zoe must have kept it to herself. Well, she'd told her kids, and they'd refused to see Pete again, which was a shame, because Genevieve had looked forward to the times he took them out so she could get a bit of peace and be by herself.

She curled her legs up on the sofa and cringed at the sound of the key going in the lock. She was going to tell him to pack his bags and go, that it was over. She'd say she was a prostitute, that he'd had sloppy seconds on many an occasion, that'd send him running.

He stumbled into the living room and slouched against the wall by the door, out of breath. "Fuck me, someone just chased after me when I left the Seven Bells. A right big bastard with a ginger beard."

She tutted. "Why? What did you do?"

"I don't know, do I! Fucking hell!"

She was going to blurt it. Now.

"I work for Debbie," she said, wanting this over with.

"So? Why do I need to know your boss' name?"

"Not just any old Debbie. Debbie from The Angel."

He blinked, uncomprehending, probably so sozzled her words didn't compute.

"I'm a prosser," she clarified.

He laughed, his hair rubbing on the wall. "Pack it in. Like I'm going to believe that after everything you said about Zoe doing it."

"You'd better believe it, because I'm not joking. I've been doing it for a while now. Shagged you plenty of times after other men have fucked me."

"That's not funny."

"I'm not trying to be."

His face contorted, and he didn't look like Pete anymore but a crazed monster. "You fucking *bitch*!"

He pushed off the wall and lunged for her, hands outstretched, reaching, probably wanting to strangle her. She jumped off the sofa, running into the kitchen and grabbing a knife, out of breath, her mind spinning then settling on a firm decision:

If he came anywhere near her, she'd kill him.

To be continued in *Ribbons*, The Cardigan Estate 18